Garbage Love

"You're always one decision
away from a different life."

Stew Hanley

Contents

Osana & Carlo

Osana always longed for a better life, yet, at the age of nineteen she falls in love with Carlo, a young auto mechanic. They grew up in the same impoverished neighborhood in the Bronx. Living with only a few city blocks between them, they likely crossed paths numerous times without notice. His hands and clothes are always covered with grease, and his arms are full of tattoos. But his blue eyes are gentle and warm, despite his party-boy reputation. Osana knows about Carlo's "love 'em and leave 'em" attitude with past girlfriends which influences her opinion of him. Their next meeting will change everything, however.

Carlo walks back to the shop from buying his uncle's lunch when he sees Osana. She is struggling with two heavy grocery bags on the other side of the street. He approaches her with a friendly smile. "Looks like you could use some help." Osana looks up, still trying to gain control over her packages, and their eyes meet for the first time.

This simple act sparks something within them—a chemistry they cannot ignore. Osana begins thinking of Carlo all the time, going out of her way to walk by his shop to give him a passing smile. Carlo finds himself looking forward to these moments.

Weeks go by, their paths cross more frequently and Osana forgets his reputation. Their conversations start with small talk but soon delve into dreams and hopes. As they indulge in beer and weed together Carlo talks about his 'big plans' for the future, and Osana shares her yearnings for a better life. The connection between them grows deeper and more serious.

One evening Carlo invites Osana to his apartment. It is furnished with second-hand items and movie posters taped to the walls. Osana barely notices, being with Carlo is all that matters. The more time they spend together, the more intimate they become. After a few months, Osana becomes pregnant, and Carlo promises to care for her and their baby. The two of them cannot be happier. Osana even begins eating healthier and does her best to abstain from alcohol and smoking weed.

Carlo excitedly goes to tell his uncle the good news about the baby. Before he gets a chance, his uncle informs him the shop is closing and he is retiring back to his home country. Carlo is devastated. This could not be happening at a worse time.

Osana is just as frustrated to hear the news, but Carlo scours the neighborhood and beyond for a new job. For weeks Carlo returns to her each night with bad news - there are no jobs available. He feels the pressure intensify as Osana's belly grows.

During a chance encounter a friend of Carlo's tells him many people are moving to Texas. According to him, there are so many jobs there aren't enough people to fill them, especially for people with mechanical skills.

This is all Carlo needs to hear. That night he fills Osana's head with fanciful visions and she agrees to go with him. She has mixed feelings about leaving the neighborhood but is assured this is the start of her better life. A place where her child can grow up free of all the hard times and negativities she had to go through.

☙❦☙

They pack what they can into Carlo's car and head to Texas. At first, they stay in a small, dated motel along what used to be a major thoroughfare. She is faithful to Carlo, sober most of the time, and focuses on preparing to be the best mother she can be.

Within a week Carlo finds a job performing maintenance and repairs on long-distance tractor-trailers just as anticipated. Osana is ecstatic; their fresh start seems to be working out perfectly.

On his first day, Carlo is anxious, but his co-workers give him a pleasant welcome and even buy him lunch. He enjoys the work and learns about large diesel engines, which he is quick to pick up on.

At quitting time on a Friday, Carlo is asked by some of the guys to go out for a few beers. Carlo agrees, missing his nights out back in the Bronx.

The bar is lively, filled with laughter and music. Before Carlo knows it, he fits right in. As the night progresses, things take another turn. Raymond from the group leans into Carlo. "You only like drinking, no weed, right?"

Carlo looks at him knowingly. "No bro, I like to smoke, too."

"Cool, I thought so." Raymond smiles and unfolds his hand to show Carlo three marijuana joints.

Carlo's eyes open wide. "Oh sweet. Where can we go?"

Raymond brings Carlo and a couple co-workers into the parking lot where they smoke weed and finish their beers. Nights like this increased from just Fridays to nearly every night in no time.

☙❦☙

As the baby's delivery date nears Carlo stays home at night more often, at Osana's insistence. Late on a Thursday night, Carlo is relaxing drinking a beer on the bed when Osana comes rushing out of the bathroom. "Honey! Honey! We gotta go to the hospital!"

"Wait. What? You're having the baby now? Like right now?" Carlo knows this is the moment they are waiting for but seems caught off-guard by the news.

"Yeah, it's coming. Hurry up!"

"Oh shit! Let me get the car." Carlo scrambles to find his keys.

"I'll get my bag and shit." Osana frantically grabs the bag she prepared and a few pieces of clothing.

Carlo runs out to the parking lot and brings the car around to the front of their unit. Osana jumps in and they take off to the hospital. Osana is so excited she cannot stop talking, giving Carlo directions to the hospital.

The dream comes to a sudden end when Carlo is pulled over for what should have been a routine traffic stop. Carlo tells the officer this is an emergency; they are heading to the hospital to have a baby. The officer immediately radios for an ambulance.

A puzzled Carlo tells the officer. "It's ok, I can bring her. We ain't got time for this!"

"You ain't going nowhere, boy. I can smell the alcohol on your breath." The officer is sharp with Carlo.

Osana is panicking; her mind and body whip between her labor pains and trying to figure out what is going on with Carlo and the officer.

The officer leans in the car window to address Osana. "Sit tight, little lady. They'll be here in two minutes." He backs up and glares at Carlo. "You, get out of the vehicle."

Carlo knows he has been drinking, reluctantly he complies with the hard-nosed officer. As they start the field sobriety tests the ambulance arrives and Osana, trembling, begins walking towards it. "I'm going now, babe. Cooperate and meet me at the hospital as soon as you can." Osana instructs him through her tears.

"Don't worry. I'll take care of this fuckin' guy and be right there!"

Carlo knows this is a lie. He does miserably with every test and is placed in handcuffs. The officer also finds a fair amount of marijuana stuffed in Carlo's right boot adding to the charges. He is brought to the police station and processed. His car is impounded and sits in the police lot waiting to be auctioned off.

A Baby Is Born

In the early morning, after hours of demanding labor, Osana gives birth to their daughter, supported by a team of strangers as Carlo sits in a jail cell down the street.

She is overjoyed holding her baby, and for the first time in her life, she feels optimistic for the future. Osana aches for her daughter to never experience the bleakness she grew up in.

Still believing Carlo received a simple ticket, Osana expects him to walk into her hospital room any minute to share in her happiness. By the afternoon, she realizes this is not going to happen. Tears roll down her face and is not sure if they are happy or sad tears. But she knows she is not alone; she has someone else to take care of this time. Osana names her Amy because no one in her family has that name. Somehow, she thinks it will distance her from the family legacy of poverty, drug abuse, and sex work.

She cannot help but feel let down. The man she loves, who promised to give her a stable life has been torn from her. After the initial shock of her life being derailed, she realizes she has no idea of how to come back from this misfortune. She does not even know how she is going to get back to the motel.

O sana lay drained in the stillness of the maternity ward listening to the beeping monitors and the shuffle of passersby in the hallway. Her only pleasure is cradling a tiny, swaddled baby in her arms. Osana cannot help but stare at Amy, her heart full of love.

A woman in her late thirties appears at the doorway to her room holding two large shopping bags, her name tag reads 'Susan.' "Mind if I come in?" Her warm smile immediately puts Osana at ease.

"Sure, sure. Please come in." Osana says eagerly.

"How's the new mom doing today?" Susan asks, walking over to the bedside.

"I'm okay," Osana replies quietly. She shifts herself in the bed to sit up more, adjusting the baby in her arms. "Still tired... but she's perfect."

Susan sees the exhaustion in Osana's face. "She is perfect, and you're doing a great job. It's not easy being a new mom."

"I don't know. I want to be a good mom, but I don't know if I can give her everything she needs. I think I might be doing it on my own now."

Susan's face shows she is unclear. "Why do you say that?"

"We got pulled over by the cops last night on the way here and my stupid finance must have got arrested. He's still ain't here."

"Well, I can tell you," Susan reassures her. "Sometimes we can't figure it all out at once, but the path you need to take will come."

Osana's eyes brighten with those words, and her tension lessens somewhat.

"You're already doing great by being here, by giving her all the love you have." Susan continues. "But there are people, like me, who are here to help you with resources, support, and the tools you need to take care of yourself and your baby. It's okay to ask for help."

"Thank you. Where I come from asking for help is a weakness. I feel like I should do everything on my own."

Susan smiles. "I know that feeling all too well. Asking for help doesn't make you weak, it makes you smart." Susan places the shopping bags on the small table in the room and takes the items out one by one showing them to Osana, explaining as she goes. Osana has just about everything she needs to take care of the little one and herself for quite a while, even a gift card to help with food or incidentals.

They sit in silence for a few moments, with only the baby's gentle cooing filling the space. "I think I'm scared." Osana admits, her voice almost a whisper.

Susan leans forward, her tone soothing. "It's okay to be scared. Everyone is at some point. But you're not alone in this. I'm here to make sure you have what you need. If you need help with childcare, with finances, with finding a job, we'll work together and figure it out."

"Am I going to be here, though?" Osana questions. "I'm not even sure what's gonna happen tomorrow. Everything's up in the air now. I don't want to mess up anymore. I'm tired of it."

"You're not going to, Osana." Susan's voice is firm but kind. "And even if you stumble, that's okay. The important thing is that you get back up. You don't have to do it all perfectly. You just have to keep trying. It's not just you anymore."

"You're right. I want to be the best mom I can be." Osana says confidently.

ﬆﬄ

O sana is released from the hospital the next day with two bags of supplies, a stroller one of the nurses found for her and baby Amy. She makes it back to the motel by taxi and rests herself and Amy down on the bed. Thoughts run through her head. "What am I going to do now?! That fuck! Everything was going great, and he fucked it up." She decides maybe, just maybe she should get comfortable with being a failure and make the best of it.

She stands under the awning outside the motel room watching the rain come down while Amy sleeps inside. With Carlo in jail, the burden of housing and feeding herself and Amy is completely on her shoulders.

She knows Amy will be waking up soon for another feeding, so she goes back into the room and prepares Amy's formula. She heard chemicals can be passed through her mother's milk. This makes her apprehensive about breastfeeding due to her drug and alcohol use in the not-too-distant past.

After mixing the baby's formula she walks over to the motel office, where she uses the microwave to warm the mixture. This is an unpleasant occurrence due to the crude comments the older man who runs the motel regularly makes towards her. "Hey Osana, looking good today!" He looks her up and down as she enters the office. "Heard about your boyfriend. What a shame, huh?"

"Can I use the microwave, please?" Osana says, ignoring his comments.

"Sure, go right ahead. It's in the same place it always is." He continues checking her body out as she walks by. "Yep, baby comes first! But, ya know, if you ever get lonely in that room, you know where to find me."

Osana continues warming the formula without saying a word.

The old man carries on. "C'mon now, don't be shy. We're practically old friends. I can keep a secret, can't you?"

The microwave beeps and the formula is ready. Using a small towel Osana takes the bottle out and starts walking to the door to leave.

"Thanks. I gotta get back to my room." Osana says not even turning in his direction. "What a mother has to do." She whispers to herself as she unlocks the door to her unit. "Oh baby, you're awake now? Look what mommy's got for you." Osana tells Amy as she puts the television on, settles in, and feeds Amy.

When Amy is satisfied Osana gets her ready and places her in the stroller. "Time to go to the store and get something for mommy to eat."

The local grocery store is a couple of blocks away. Osana goes up and down the aisles picking up what she needs and proceeds to the checkout. The cashier is a mature woman, who has seen Osana shopping before. She eyes Osana sympathetically. "Tough times?" she asks, her voice low.

Osana nods, choking back tears. "I'm doing my best, but things just seem to--"

"Hang in there, honey. You're stronger than you think," the woman tells her. It is enough to make Osana feel a little less alone. They talk about Amy for a minute before Osana heads out.

Osana sits back in the room eating the prepared food she picked up while comforting Amy. This is her routine for quite a few nights and will be for a few more. She wonders when she will be able to pick her goals up again. A good first step, she thinks, is to find out what Carlo's situation is. She decides to visit him in jail to find out what their future looks like.

⁂

On visiting day, she gets herself and Amy ready and takes a cab over to the jailhouse. Osana has a somewhat positive outlook about this encounter during the ride.

Upon reaching the jail's security checkpoint, her attitude changes. The concrete walls give a sense of permanency, and the guards are imposing. Her hopes for a quick resolution to this impasse sink with each step. Osana fidgets with her bags nervously as she approaches the metal detectors.

"Morning." a guard greets her in a gravelly voice, looking her up and down. "You've got to empty your pockets and bags. Pass the stroller around the detectors."

Osana gestures consent, unzips her bag, and places her phone and keys in the small bin. She pushes the stroller forward, watching as the guard waves a handheld metal detector over it. Amy seems to smile at the guard as he does, innocent of the setting.

"Everything seems fine." the guard says. "Just take a seat in the waiting area."

She pushes the stroller into the waiting area, where a few other visitors sit. The room buzzes with a low hum of conversations, some laughter, but mainly quiet sadness.

Osana finds a spot and settles in, she is not sure how she feels about Carlo at this point, still deciding if she should be angry or feel sorry for him. They had spoken on the phone briefly but seeing him behind bars will make the situation undeniable.

"Is this your first visit?" a woman asks with a gentle tone in her voice.

Osana turns to her. "Yeah. I'm just... a bit nervous."

The woman smiles knowingly. "It's always hard the first time. Just remember, he'll be happy to see you both."

It feels like an eternity passes as Osana waits. She rocks Amy gently in the stroller, trying to calm her own thoughts.

Finally, a guard calls her name. "Osana?"

She stands up and pushes the stroller to the door the guard points to. She is led down a corridor, her heart pounds harder with each step.

When they arrive at the visitation room, it confirms Osana has miscalculated her optimism. The walls are stark, and the room is filled with chaotic tables lined with cheap folding chairs. "This is serious shit. He ain't getting out of here any time soon." she thinks to herself. And then, she sees Carlo sitting near the back. His appearance is like a punch to Osana's gut, but the moment Carlo spots them his face lights up.

"There's my babies!" His voice is a mixture of excitement and relief. Osana rushes over, throws her arms around his neck to feel the familiar warmth of his embrace. It is a momentary escape from the harsh reality.

Carlo leans over and kisses Amy, caressing her face for a minute. "Let me look at you, baby. I'm your daddy."

"At least you get to see her finally."

"She's so beautiful, just like her mother!" Carlo kisses Amy again. "You guys are all I think of in here."

"Yeah, well, I brought you some snacks." Osana pulls a small bag from her purse.

"You're amazing. You didn't have to." Carlo pauses for a second. "Hey, do you think you can put some money in my commissary account? Just so I can buy some razors and stuff."

"I don't have much on me, but I'll ask on my way out," she sits across from him putting the stroller between them. "How are you holding up?"

Carlo sighs, leaning back in his chair. "It ain't a day at Orchard Beach, ya know. Every day is the same shit over and over."

"Yeah, tell me about it." Osana says looking down at the table.

"Listen, babe. I might be in here for a while, so I was thinking—"

"Ain't it just like a drunk driving ticket?" she asks, already recognizing his situation is more precarious. Osana doesn't know all the charges pending against him, and Carlo does not want her to know. "But, babe, what are they charging you with? You gotta know that."

"It's like the drunk driving and some other shit." Carlo says trying to downplay his status.

"What other shit?"

"Babe, listen. I'm gonna deal with all that, it just might take a while."

Osana is frustrated by his responses. "So, what do you want me to do? I mean, I'll wait if you want."

"Nah, babe. How you gonna live out here without me? You got the baby; you can't work or nothing."

"So, go back to New York?"

"I don't want you to, but I think you gotta for now. Let me deal with this shit and I'll come get you. Ya know we can always come back here... or somewhere else if you want."

This news is the farthest thing from what Osana is expecting from today's visit. Osana's anger and resentment is growing steadily inside her. "I was hoping you get outta here in a couple days or whatever. Now it's like some open-ended shit."

"I know, but let me do what I gotta do and we can get back on track. Just go back home for a little while."

"Well, if that's what you want, I guess so." Carlo can tell Osana's tone has changed with this response.

"Babe, it'll be ok. Trust me."

"Yeah, I did trust you, and look where we are!" Osana says no longer holding back her feelings.

Carlo does his best to calm her down and switches the conversation to Amy. He asks about what she is doing and whatever cute baby stories he can get Osana to tell him.

"Ok, people, visiting time is up! We need all visitors to report back to the desk." announces the prison guard.

"Babe, please don't be mad. I didn't plan it to work out---"

"We gotta go now. Say goodbye to Amy."

Carlo comes around the table and kisses Amy and tells her he's going to miss her. He stands and embraces Osana, but she is cold and distant.

Osana grabs hold of the stroller and begins pushing it towards the exit. "Ok, baby, time to go."

"It'll be ok, Osana, you'll see." Carlo tells Osana as he turns and heads back to his cell.

As Osana walks away, she glances back one last time, catching Carlo's gaze. She contemplates if their love can endure if she returns to the Bronx and Carlo is locked up for an extended period. She returns to her motel room more disheartened than ever.

Back to The Bronx

By now money and baby supplies are running low. Osana figures she has no choice but to turn a trick, buy a bus ticket, and return to the neighborhood. As fucked up as she feels returning will be, it is familiar, her comfort zone, and appears to be her only option. She considers finding a part-time job to pay the motel bill and keep Amy and herself fed but has no friends or family around. There is no one trustworthy enough to watch Amy while she would be gone.

On her next trip to the motel office, the old man continues his sexual advances. Osana is hoping he will this time, getting her resolve up she turns to face him. "Oh yeah? What would you do if I let you?"

"I really like those big lips of yours!" he says, ogling Osana with a vile look on his face.

Osana takes a deep breath. "I need a hundred dollars."

"What? I can get five blowjobs for that!"

"Maybe, but not with me."

The old man stands there thinking for a minute until Osana interjects. "C'mon, I gotta get back to my baby before she wakes up."

"Ok...ok, fuck it." The old man reaches for a metal box under the counter takes the cash out of it and shows Osana.

"We'll go in the bathroom there." He says pointing to a door towards the back of the office.

Osana walks in after him and they close the door. The old man drops his pants and leans against the sink while Osana gets down on her knees. He only last three minutes, which Osana is grateful for. The old man fixes his pants and walks out, while Osana rinses her mouth out in the sink.

Osana grabs the baby's bottle and the cash, immediately rushing back to her room. She quickly checks on Amy, who is still sleeping, and rushes into the bathroom where she proceeds to empty her stomach into the toilet.

She sits next to the toilet bowl for a while, crying wondering how her life has become so unpleasant again. It is only Amy's cries that bring her back to some measure of composure. Osana re-heats Amy's bottle under the hot water in the bathroom sink and feeds her. After cleaning Amy up the two of them fall asleep on the bed.

Osana is awakened by the early morning sun streaming in through the broken window shade. She sits up and looks at Amy. "Well, baby, today's the day." Osana takes a fast shower and gets the two of them ready for their journey.

Carefully packing the diaper bag with bottles, fresh diapers, a soft blanket, and a couple of Amy's toys. She adds a couple of snacks for herself and zips the bag closed. The rest of Osana's items go into her small travel luggage. "Are you ready for an adventure?" Osana chuckles, glancing down at Amy, who coos in delight. Osana calls for a taxi and has mixed emotions during the cab ride; still wondering if she should wait for Carlo.

T he small bus station is busier than Osana expects, but she finds the right window and buys her ticket. Sitting on the old wooden benches, Osana keeps Amy busy with her toys while they wait for their bus.

Osana's ears pick up when she hears her bus called over the speakers. She gathers her belongings and pushes Amy to the gate. Finding a seat towards the rear of the bus, she settles in and readies Amy for the long trip.

As the bus pulls away and gets on the highway, Osana stares out the window watching the landscape change from farmland to urban scenes and back again. When the sun begins to set it casts a warm hue over everything, but Osana's attention is focused on the little bundle in her arms. Amy is nestled against Osana's shoulder, her tiny fingers curling around a brown stuffed bear Osana.

The baby's gentle breathing has a calming pattern to it, and Osana cannot help but smile at the sight of her. As serene as she is feeling now, Carlo pops in and out of her mind, but she forces herself not to think about the harm he has done. She swears to herself she will never let another man upset her life again.

This bus ride is just what she appears to need. 'God works in mysterious ways' passes through her mind as her Catholic upbringing speeds through her head.

The ride is relatively uneventful. Osana manages to keep Amy entertained with her stuffed bear, and a few other soft toys. She manages to sleep herself while the baby sleeps. But as the journey wears on, Amy begins to get restless. Her little face scrunches up in discomfort, letting out a soft whimper.

Osana places Amy against her chest and begins humming a gentle lullaby. One she makes up as she goes along. She has no recollection of anyone doing this for her, but she vows to be the mother she never had. It is not long before Amy becomes quiet, and Osana thinks she must be a natural at this.

An elderly woman sitting across the aisle notices Osana's efforts and gives her a compassionate smile. "Is she okay, dear?" she asks in a caring voice.

"Yeah, she's just a bit restless," Osana tries to sound upbeat despite her growing fatigue. "It's a long ride, that's all."

The woman reaches into her bag and pulls out a small package of crackers. "Here, try giving her some of these. It might help settle her." Osana takes the crackers gratefully. "Thank you so much." Osana knows she cannot give them to her newborn and eats them herself when the elderly woman closes her eyes.

Osana is fond of looking into the windows of the passing cars wondering if they are happy and have good mothers. Or if they are they are broke and miserable. Of course, she will never know, but she thinks she has a good sense by looking at their faces.

As night sets in, Osana considers what her mother is going to think of her showing up with a baby, her granddaughter. Will she be excited and welcome them into her home, be indifferent, or reject them completely. She will soon have her answer.

Amy drifts off to sleep again, her tiny breaths warm against Osana's neck. The motion of the bus seems to lull her into a quiet slumber, and Osana feels a quiet serenity. She gets herself into a position to sleep, careful not to disturb Amy. Osana does what she can to get through the many stops the bus makes, the mind-numbing hours and two long nights on the bus.

As daylight comes the landscape becomes familiar. The skyscrapers of New York City are in view. Osana wonders what this chapter of her life will bring with each mile they drive. As the bus pulls into the Port Authority bus station in Manhattan, she gathers her things and readies Amy. She steps off the bus, her heart swells with anticipation.

She still needs to go downstairs and get the #2 subway train up to Hunts Point and the bus over to her mom's building. All in all, she does this with relative ease. She has been on mass transit many times, but never with a baby and all the trappings.

N early three days after leaving Texas she knocks on her mother's apartment door. Three knocks bring no response from inside, but a woman from the next unit appears on the fourth. She informs Osana her mother has not been there for three months and heard she might not be back for a long time. "Maybe she got arrested again?" the neighbor says, not to embarrass Osana, but they both know that is exactly what happened.

This is so disappointing Osana does not want to know the details. She knows there is nothing she can do about it anyway. It is best to move on. If and when her mother returns, she will see her then.

The neighbor tells Osana she grabbed some items while the superintendent was clearing out the apartment she thought her mother might want to keep.

"That was nice, thanks." Osana tells her.

"I have two boxes in my apartment if you want to look through them, some of it may be yours. The woman offers nosily.

Osana stands there thinking if this is something she really wants to do. "Yeah, I'm here; mind as well look." And she is thankful she did because inside the second box are three small paintings she did as a young girl. "Oh wow!" Osana's face lights up as she pulls them out. "I can't believe she still has these."

"I'm so happy I kept them. I wasn't sure what was important or not." The neighbor exclaims. "I like the ones with the dogs."

"Yeah, we had two when I was a kid. The other's just some trees in a forest."

"I think they're very nice. You must have been talented."

"Right, used to be." Osana says regrettably. "Thanks for grabbing this stuff."

Osana places the paintings with her other belongings and says goodbye. Osana and Amy head a couple of blocks over and ring the bell of Osana's old friend Bella.

※※※

B ella is heard over the intercom. "Who's this?"

"It's Sana, stupid!" Osana gives the nickname her friends call her.

"Oh, my bitch." Bella shouts happily. "When did you get back?"

"C'mon, buzz me in and I'll tell you the whole story!"

The door buzzes and up go Osana and Amy. Bella is leaning out her open apartment door as Osana gets off the elevator.

"Oh my god! Let me see that baby!" The two hug for a while and finally separate when Bella starts talking. "Come in, come in."

"Yeah, I gotta put this stuff down!"

"Let me see her."

"She's perfect, Sana. Absolutely perfect."

Osana agrees with tears welling up in her eyes. "I can't believe it. She's actually here. It feels like a dream."

Bella reaches out and gently touches the baby's hand. "Look at her little fingers. She's already holding onto me."

Osana giggles. "Yeah, she's making herself known. I keep wondering how I got so lucky."

"So, this is Carlo's baby?" Bella asks quietly.

"Yep."

"Should I ask where he is?"

"Maybe later. How about you? No babies yet?"

"Nope, no babies. Plenty of fucking, though!" Bella says flippantly.

"Ha! You'll never change!"

"Why should I? Let the good times roll!"

"I just had a baby, so the good times are gonna have to wait a while." Osana informs her, adjusting herself in the seat.

"Still sore down there, huh? You got plenty of time, don't worry." Bella crouches down to Amy. "But look at her. She's so tiny and full of potential. What's her name?"

"Amy."

"Amy? After who?"

"After nobody. That's the point."

"Oh, I got you. Amy, beautiful. It suits her."

Osana is touched. "Thank you. It kinda feels good to be back home, even though I don't actually have a home."

"What do you mean?"

"I'm all alone, Bella. I just found out my mother is gone, too."

"I just saw her recently!"

"Her neighbor said she's been gone for a few months."

"Yeah, now that I think about it, it might be that long. You're never alone, Osana. Not with me around!"

"And Amy?"

"She's gonna have both of us to spoil her! Stay here for a while until you get straightened out."

Osana smiles through her tears. "Thank you, Bella. That means the world to me – to us." looking at the baby.

"Are you kidding, it's so boring around here. I need you guys around, too."

Bella goes to the refrigerator and cracks open two bottles of beer, handing one to Osana. "To Amy. And to us."

Osana agrees and takes a sip of beer. The two women share a heartfelt hug, their eyes never leaving the baby. The room is filled with a sense of hope and love, a new chapter beginning with Amy at the center.

Osana takes a long drink of beer "Ah, that's nice. I haven't had a cold one in a while."

"Yeah, but I can't smoke weed in here anymore. The old fuck next door called the cops on me, and nobody needs that shit. Maybe later we can take a walk and smoke. Ya know, if the baby's sleeping or whatever." Bella takes a swig of beer. "So... tell me. What happened to Carlo? I thought you two were so lovey-dovey?"

"Yeah, we were. Until the dumb shit got arrested for drinking and some other shit."

"That fuck!"

"Yeah, in Texas of all places; I ain't hanging around for that. He probably had warrants, too, so who knows how long he'll be locked up."

"Ugh, that sucks."

Osana pauses for a few seconds. "Thanks for letting me stay here, really."

"Don't get mushy on me now. I only got the one bedroom, but you can sleep with me or out here if you want." Bella offers.

"Sleep with you? On those stained sheets? How many guys--"

"Listen you, I change those sheets all the time!"

O sana stays with her friend while she applies for her social service benefits. She could get her own apartment when those come through. They spend most of their time and money Bella earns from turning tricks, on alcohol and drugs. Weed and beer are their two drugs of choice. They do not shy away from harder drugs when they get the opportunity, though.

Through all this Osana focuses on obtaining her new life and home. Osana, with Amy in tow, arrives at the social services office after a tiring bus ride. She spent much of her life navigating the city's labyrinth of bureaucracy, so she has a good understanding of how to play the game.

Osana feels a certain sadness walking to the office needing to apply for these benefits, but dreams Amy will never have to. She leans into the stroller and says, "When you grow up be smart and make a lot of money, baby." Reaching the office Osana takes a seat in one of the hard plastic chairs with Amy now in her arms. The waiting area is full of people staring at their phones or shuffling papers.

When it's her turn Osana approaches the counter where an aloof-looking woman sits, typing away at a computer. "Excuse me," Osana says, "I'm here to apply for benefits."

The woman turns from her computer screen. "What kind of benefits you looking for?"

"The supplemental nutrition program for my baby, housing assistance, and unemployment for me. I can't work." Osana answers.

The woman nods, sliding applications toward her. "Here's WIC, SNAP, and here's the cash assistance. Fill them out and bring them back to me when you're done. It might take a while to process. And you might get a follow-up call and some paperwork." Her voice is flat and unemotional from uttering this same message so many times before.

"Thanks." Osana says. She takes the papers and sits down again, putting Amy back in her stroller. She fills everything out while Amy amuses herself. Osana picks her head up from time to time to look at Amy and the folks sitting around her. She feels the pressure of making ends meet while trying to build a future for her baby. She curses Carlo under her breath for putting her in this situation.

Osana puts her pen away and stands up, her legs and back stiff from sitting so long. She walks to the counter and hands the forms back as instructed. The woman takes them and places the paperwork on the lofty pile of applications next to her. "Ok, you'll get a call and have your interview next week." Osana says thank you quietly, steps off to the side and gets Amy ready for the bus ride back home. "We're gonna be ok." she whispers buttoning Amy's sweater.

Osana's benefits come through some weeks later and she announces to Bella. "You know you're my bestie and I love you, but I can't stand living with you!"

"Same here, bitch. Pack your shit up and get the fuck out!" Bella says laughingly.

Osana does not have much more than a suitcase or so worth of belongings to move. When moving day comes, they hug and cry a bit, but know they going to see each other often.

A New Home

O sana and Amy relocate to an apartment only three blocks away from Bella's. It is a nice place with a good layout and the landlord made repairs before their moving in. The building has fourteen other units, but Osana snubs all of them because of past negative experiences, or just 'bad vibes' she gets from them. She does sense a fellowship with Elvie from the apartment right next to hers.

Elvie is an older woman who spent her life in the neighborhood, except for short-term prison sentences for prostitution and drug possession. She transformed herself through self-discovery but carries the scars of her former life. Elvie's journey from addiction to recovery has instilled a deep sense of empathy in her. This makes her an invaluable asset to the women's shelter where she volunteers. She chooses to live a calm, quiet life by herself and two cats – Kitti and Tracey.

"Welcome to the building, dear." Elvie greets Osana as they meet in the hallway.

"Oh, thank you!" Osana responds.

"What's your name? And who's this little one?"

"I'm Osana and that's my daughter, Amy."

"She's so cute!" Elvie whispers as she peeks into the stroller.

"Thank you. I like to think so."

"She really is. I'm Elvie, I live next door. Your apartment should be in pretty good shape. The old miser who owns this place finally spent some money in there."

"Yeah, I saw some guys working when I looked at the place."

"They were working for a few weeks. I know because they woke me up every morning! I even saw them bringing in new appliances."

"Nice, I didn't know that. Well, I'd better get in and start figuring out what I need."

"Yes, make it yours! By the way, if my gospel music is too loud you just bang on the wall, and I'll lower it. Oh, and I'm home most days and every night so if you ever need a babysitter, I'm right here."

"Ok, thanks." Osana continues down to her door.

Elvie stands there assessing Osana before returning to her apartment. Osana reminds her of herself from years ago. Elvie discerns Osana thinks she is doing just fine hiding all her habits, but the signs are obvious. Osana is young and pretty, but Elvie can see the wear and tear of drinking and drug use on Osana's face. The subtle signs in her speech and mannerisms show she is just another run-of-the-mill product of the neighborhood.

Osana opens the apartment door, steps in, and looks around. As she does, she thinks this is going to be her sanctuary; there is not going to be any craziness. She understands her friends will be partying there occasionally, but those times will happen within clear-cut controls. She tells herself if she 'entertains' chosen male friends for monetary reasons that will be under strict guidelines, too. She promises herself to keep her life as low-key as possible from now on.

She uses her benefits wisely, purchases a nice bedroom, kitchen, and living room sets, and even mounts her paintings in a prominent place. She spends the most money and attention in Amy's room. All these new purchases have created quite a pile of cardboard boxes and packing materials.

"Who the hell is yelling down there?" Osana utters as she steps towards her apartment window.

"Yo Jimmy, c'mon! Who gives a shit what's in the cans. Let's go!" Danny shouts from the cab of a sanitation truck.

"Fuck, another rat! I swear I'm seeing more and more of these little bastards!" his co-worker Jimmy exclaims.

Danny laughs. "Maybe if you didn't poke around the cans the buggers wouldn't jump out at you. You think you're going to find a pot of gold?"

"You Irish prick! I found that toolbelt you love so much, didn't I?"

"Ok, ok you finished, my love?"

"Yeah, next stop funny guy." Jimmy hops back on the truck as it pulls away.

"Shit, I missed the truck again!" Osana says annoyed. "I have so much shit to throw out. I'm sick of looking at it."

Osana finishes dressing and decides what she wants for breakfast. She puts Amy in the stroller, and they head to the corner grocery store. After picking up baby formula, a couple breakfast items for her, and two quarts of beer she proceeds to the cashier. She thumps her items and a twenty-dollar bill down on the counter. The cashier rings her up as he bags and says. "Thank you."

"Hey, that's not twenty bucks!" Osana hollers.

"I'm putting the change towards the forty you owe me!" the cashier snaps back.

"Oh c'mon, I need that money. I'll give you the whole thing next time, I swear."

"You know how many people tell me that shit?"

"There's other stores around here, ya know… so fuck you!" She snatches her bags off the counter and exits, spewing profanities.

As she walks to her apartment building, she sees Bella walking down the block. As they get closer Osana shouts. "You got?"

"Would I be there if I didn't?" Bella answers.

"Cool, let's get upstairs. I got us a couple quarts, too."

"Are they cold this time?"

"Fuck off! The warm ones are cheaper!"

"You cheap bitch! You'd rather save fifty cents and give your bestie a warm beer?"

"Haha, you know it! More money for the important shit." Osana looks down at what Bella is wearing. It is more out-landish than her usual colorful mix of odd finds and eclectic accessories. "And what the fuck are you even wearing?"

"What? This? looking down at herself. "It reveals my daz-zling personality, girl!"

"It's revealing, all right. You're too much!"

"My dad got this for me. How bad can it be?"

They laugh as they walk up two flights to the apartment. Bella's comment about her father strikes a chord in Osana for an instant. Her father was shot and killed in a street fight just two weeks after her birth. The few stories her mother told her are all she ever knew of him.

The Meeting

One morning, as Osana throws out more cardboard boxes from her deliveries, the sanitation truck with Jimmy and Danny rolls up.

"So, you're the one with all the boxes!" Jimmy exclaims as he hops off the back of the truck.

"Guilty!" Osana replies. "Ain't it ok?"

"Yeah, sure, sure." Jimmy says then pauses. "Well, they should really be put out on Wednesdays, that's recycling day."

"Sorry, I didn't know."

"It's fine. We'll take it anyway. I wouldn't want to disappoint such a beautiful woman like yourself."

Osana feigns a giggle. "Thanks. I'm just trying to clean up my apartment."

"That's cool. I didn't catch your name."

"It's Osana."

"Wow, that's a beautiful name. Does it mean anything?"

"Yeah, like god save us or something." Osana replies nonchalantly.

"Well, we can all use some of that. I'm Jimmy, by the way. You just move in?"

"Not long ago."

"Well, welcome to the neighborhood, I guess."

"Do you live around here?" Osana asks.

"No, I'm in Pelham Bay, kind of far."

"Yo Jimmy, we're three blocks behind!" Danny shouts from the front of the truck.

As Jimmy empties the rest of the garbage cans into the truck, he turns to Osana, "He's such an ass! Anyway, it was great meeting you. See you next time!"

Jimmy jumps back into position on the truck, and it slowly rolls away. All the while Jimmy keeps his eyes on Osana, and she watches him for a few seconds. Her mind is going back and forth between him being a nerd or a potential source of funds at some point, mostly the latter. Her gaze doesn't last long as she turns and goes back into the building.

Danny is a veteran of the Sanitation Department, and he loves every minute of it. A large, strapping Irishman from the 'other side,' he is well-suited for physical labor and working outside. Getting to the bar by 5:00 p.m. is an added perk he savors. He loves being the life of the party, although he has never shied away from a fight.

Jimmy typically works the back of the truck emptying the garbage cans set out the night before. While not slight, he is not as well-matched for this line of work. He is physically capable but does not fancy sanitation work as Danny does. His mind is always working on other things, some good and some not-so-good. A 'good guy' by most accounts, but he feels he never fits into any situation completely. Growing up in an old-fashioned immigrant household, he strives to do what is expected of him.

After their last pick-up, Jimmy joins Danny in the cab. "She's pretty hot, no?"

Danny is baffled. "Who ya talking about, lad?

"The young one with all the boxes. The one I was talking to."

"Oh yeah, yeah. She's all right."

"She is better than that, c'mon Danny. Slim and young with that jet black hair." Jimmy says spiritedly. "And you didn't see her from behind. That ass is incredible!"

"So, what? You wanna bang her now?" Danny says mockingly.

"What? No way."

"Ah, c'mon. I wouldn't blame ya. You sound really into her."

"Dude, it's called being nice. A nasty prick like you wouldn't know anything about it."

"Yeah, yeah. You're always thinking about banging someone. I don't blame you, but you get emotionally attached to these hoes. Remember last time? You went a little nuts and I had to reel you back in. They're just hoes. I grab a BJ from one of the bar sluts once in a while, but that's it, then I go home."

"Yeah, home to yourself. I was just fuckin' around with her. That's all. You gotta make something out of everything?"

"Ok, fine. Whatever you say, my friend. How 'bout a beer after work?"

"Nope, I can't tonight.

"You never can, lad. What the fuck?"

"I know, but Marie wants me to pick up the baby's test results on the way home and they close early. She's gotta bring them to the other doctor tomorrow."

"Right, how's the little girl doing?"

"About the same. They still don't know what's going on with her. It's her heart, so she's just like weak all the time. Marie is worried about her."

"I'm praying for her, man. All you guys."

"Thanks, Danny."

"And how's the boy doing?"

"Yeah, he's fine. He started kindergarten this year and seems to love it; always bringing home artwork they did, shit like that."

"That's great. I remember those days. Good memories. My two guys are twenty-five and twenty-nine years old. I only hear from them when they need money."

Jimmy laughs. "Yeah, I guess that's what I have to look forward to."

After some talk about politics and sports, they pull into the depot and Danny drives circling the yard slowly. "These assholes park their fuckin' trucks all over the place!"

Jimmy looks around. "Someone's in your spot."

"That's fuckin' Louie. He does that shit on purpose!"

"Gee, I'd love to stay and hear you piss and moan, but I gotta go, Danny."

"Alright, no problem. I'll take care of this."

Jimmy jumps out of the cab and walks over to his car. As he is about to open the car door he hears Mark, his supervisor, call his name. Jimmy turns around and sees Mark walking towards him.

Mark is the kind of man who blends into the background of nearly every setting. For his office being amid a sanitation yard it is neat and organized. He is a low-level supervisor in the department with many duties and a large staff to manage. At its core, his role is to ensure that everything is in its right place at the right time and none of the workers get out of line. Despite how mundane his role is, Mark takes his job seriously.

"Hey Jimmy, how's it going?"

"Yeah, not bad, Mark. How 'bout you?"

"Same shit, Jimmy. Ya know."

"Is everything ok?" Jimmy asks.

"Oh yeah. I heard your little one was sick. Is she better now?"

"Actually no. She's still not well. She was born with a heart condition, so she's very frail and needs a lot of attention all the time."

"I'm sorry. I didn't hear all that. How's your wife dealing with it?"

"Marie's the one taking care of her mostly. The baby's out of the hospital, but my wife spends a lot of time on her. We got a 5-year-old boy, too, but he's in good shape."

"I know we ain't been best buddies or anything, but if there's anything I can do to help please let me know."

"I appreciate it, Mark. Thank you. They tell us there's a lot of babies with this defect who grow up with normal lives, so we're hopeful."

"Well, that's good news. I'll be praying for her."

"Actually, I gotta go pick up some test results for her right now really, so--"

"Oh, sorry, Jimmy. Yeah, go ahead."

"Thanks, Mark, for everything."

As Jimmy drives his mind starts racing again. He can't decipher what he is even thinking about when this happens. It seems too much to process - Marie, the kids, the job, but particularly the image of Osana's ass in those sweatpants - rush through his brain. He gets to the imaging center and rushes in. "Hi, I gotta pick up my daughter's scan thing."

"What's the name?"

"Sorry, Rizzo. Jeannie Rizzo."

"Yes, I have them right here." The receptionist hands a large manila folder over the counter to him.

"Thanks. Anything I should know about?"

"You'll have to ask the doctor."

"But are they good or bad?"

"Sir, I can't give you any information."

Jimmy is annoyed but says "Ok, I get it." as he turns to head out.

Back in the car, he is feeling more overwhelmed as he starts to drive home. He's not even sure how he made it as he pulls up to his apartment building. He takes a minute to calm down, so he can play his part before getting upstairs.

"Marie, I'm here."

Marie emerges out of the bedroom shushing Jimmy to be quiet. "I just got her to sleep."

"Sorry." He hands her the envelope he picked up. "I asked if they had any information--"

"They won't tell you anything. We have to bring it to the doctor."

"Yeah, I know that now. When you bringing her?"

"Tomorrow at 10."

"Why are the appointments always early? I gotta work and going in late is a problem."

"It's ok. You don't need to be there. I'll take care of it... as usual." Marie replies in a passive-aggressive tone.

"Don't say it like that. It's not like I don't want to go."

"Yeah, I know. You just always have to--"

"Work... I know... I gotta work." Jimmy thinks this is yet another dig he must stand there and take it like an idiot.

"Where's my boy?" Jimmy asks, trying to lighten the tone of the exchange.

"In his bedroom. He's got homework to do."

"Are they up to algebra yet?" Jimmy asks sarcastically.

"Yeah, right. They give them some letters to copy and stuff."

Jimmy walks around her and heads to Bobby's bedroom. "Hey, my boy! What 'cha doing?"

"My homework."

"Perfect! You gonna grow up to be a smart guy and make a lot of money, right?"

"Mommy says I should do good and get a job more better than yours."

Jimmy stands there irritated, looking at his son not knowing how to react. "Well, sometimes grow-ups gotta do what they gotta do. You'll learn that when you get older. Whatever you do I'll be proud of you."

"Thanks, daddy."

"Remember I always love you no matter what. Let me know if you need help." Jimmy pats Bobby on the head and goes back to the kitchen.

"Thanks for that, Marie."

"For what?"

"Telling Bobby my job sucks."

"I didn't tell him that! What'd he say?"

"You said he's got to grow up and get a better job than me." Jimmy conveys in a fatigued tone.

"I just said he should study and get a good job, that's all."

"I don't know, but that's not the way it took it."

"I wouldn't know about that."

"No, of course not. What else is new." Jimmy tired of this exchange looks around the kitchen. "What are we eating any-way?"

Marie gladly switches subjects. "I made veal cutlets. They're almost ready."

"Cool, that's good. Let's eat." Calls Bobby from the living room "C'mon. Dinner time."

"Didn't I just tell you the baby was sleeping, to be quiet?"

"Sorry, I forgot."

Jimmy sits at the dining room table eating trying to stay included in the conversation. It is the usual banter about the baby, money, and the details of their lives. To Jimmy, they run through the same topics each evening with no direction or purpose. There was a time when it was simply boring to him, but recently it has become increasingly mind-numbing. He is starting to understand it is not only his family making this way, but life in general. As this awareness grows, so does his frustration.

Afterward, Marie goes into her usual routine of feeding the baby, getting Bobby ready for bed, and fussing around the place. Jimmy spends this time sitting on the couch watching the news, trying to keep his mind in check. At last, it is the hour he waits for – bedtime.

He climbs into bed with Marie, who is already half sleeping and kisses her good night. As she does most nights, she rolls over and puts her back to him. He gets 'that feeling' come over him again. He is unsure if he wants to scream or cry, but does neither. He only lays there hoping someone or something would fill this emptiness inside him.

A Flawed Start

The next morning Jimmy goes about his usual routine as quietly as possible. He leaves for work early and tries not to wake anyone. Not out of any thoughtfulness, he just doesn't want to deal with any of the prattle the family might bring up. In his mind, he has to deal with 'garbage' all day at work, so he wants to keep hearing it to a minimum at home.

Danny approaches Jimmy waiting at their truck. "Ah, it's a great day for taking out the trash, wouldn't you say, Jimmy?"

"Whatever you say, Danny." Jimmy forces out.

Danny adds "Maybe you'll find that pot of gold today!"

"Hopefully I'll find something." Jimmy says to himself out loud.

They spend their morning just like all the others. Driving up and down the same tired blocks, stopping frequently to empty the cans – over and over. Jimmy wonders how Danny is not fed up with this after twenty-two years. He reminds himself he should study for one of the civil service promotion tests and get off the trucks. But is annoyed when he remembers he's been thinking that for years now.

Days go by without a single detail to differentiate one day from the day before. Jimmy is becoming more depressed and is losing track of time. Until the day his heart starts to beat again. They turn the corner to go down Osana's block, and Jimmy's eyes widen. He swears he sees Osana outside of her building. He wants to shout for Danny to hurry up, but he does not want the mocking he will have to endure for asking.

They are only two stops away and Jimmy does his best to wave so she would notice, to no avail. She throws a trash bag in the can and walks back into the building, not even looking his way. And off Jimmy and Danny go to the next stop and next block and next street.

This happens twice more over the coming weeks and Jimmy is getting more single-minded about meeting her. Then it happens. She is at the trash cans and looks in Jimmy's direction. He waves and she waves back before returning inside. But they made eye contact and Jimmy believes there is some sort of chemistry.

Jimmy is very pleased with this. In his mind, it was a 'good day' and made 'good progress.' He gets his hopes up more than ever. He is looking forward to going to work now, which amazes him. 'So, this is what it takes, huh?' he laughs to himself.

About a week later, just as the truck is pulling up to her building, Osana emerges pushing her daughter in a stroller. Jimmy jumps off the truck and starts emptying the cans. "Hey, good morning!"

"Good morning." Osana answers blandly.

"Taking the little one for a walk?"

"Yeah, something like that."

"Cool. Can I talk to you a minute? Like over here." Jimmy says pointing to a spot near the curb.

"What? I gotta go." But she lets go of the stroller and walks a few feet over to Jimmy.

"I just wanted to ask if you knew who keeps throwing the crack vials and drug stuff out in the garbage. The cops may notice one day and start asking about it."

Osana fakes getting upset at the question knowing it is probably from her apartment. "What the hell are you asking me for? I don't know!"

"I didn't mean anything by it. I didn't think it was you. You're just the first-"

Osana marches over to the stroller and storms off.

"I'm a fuckin' idiot! Of all the shit I could have said I picked that." Jimmy mutters and proceeds to beat himself up over it for days. He realizes he needs to plan first, not improvise if he is going to gain her affection. He ponders the situation, running various scenarios in his mind. For one thing, the plan had to take place without Danny around. He needs more time to talk with her and it would be best if she didn't have the daughter with her. After work would not be a good opportunity. Osana probably settles in her apartment and does not go out, and he needs to get home. It would have to be on one of his days off.

"Yes, that's it" Jimmy realizes. "I'll take the car, sit up near the grocery store they all go to, and she'll probably run out on a Saturday morning to buy something."

For three Saturdays he wakes up early and gives his wife some bullshit story about starting to shoot hoops with the guys again or some other flimsy excuse to get out of the apartment. He presumes Marie has some inkling something is going on, but he is so focused on his objective he doesn't care.

※ ※ ※

Jimmy sees Osana walking towards the grocery store through his windshield on the fourth Saturday. He waits until she gets into the store, exits his car, and walks in himself. He goes up and down the small aisles until he sees her. "Hey, I know you!" he approaches her.

"Who? Oh, you?" Osana says slightly unnerved by his appearance.

"Yeah, just me. I wanted to apologize for the last time we met. I really didn't mean anything--"

"What'd you say? I don't remember." Osana says with a baffled look. "Just forget it. Really. What are you doing here around here?"

"I was just driving through and wanted to get a bottle of water." Jimmy steps over and grabs one out of the refrigerated case. He notices she has some breakfast items and a six-pack of beer in her arms.

"You ready to check out?"

"Um, I guess." They start walking towards the front of the store.

"Well, can I make it up to you by paying for your stuff?"

The offer strikes a certain chord in Osana, and she again sees him as a source of cash. "Sure, why not. What's your name again?"

"Jimmy. Thanks."

They put their items up on the counter together, and the cashier asks if he's paying for everything.

"Yeah, I am. Ring it up together."

"You wanna pay her tab, too?"

"Shut up you little asshole!" Osana shouts at the cashier.

"Wait. She owes money?" Jimmy is not sure what just transpired.

"Don't mind him, Jimmy. He's just being a jerk."

"Jerk? She owes me forty dollars for weeks."

Jimmy turns to Osana. "No, it's fine. I want to make it up to you."

Jimmy is deliberately carrying a thick wad of cash this day. He pulls it from his pocket, making sure Osana gets a glimpse and pays for the groceries. The cashier finishes packing Osana's items and she takes her bag, Jimmy grabs his water, and the two walk out.

As they do a poorly dressed middle-aged man with straggly hair walks by. "Yo Sana! What's going on?"

"Just fine, Spark. How 'bout you?"

"Ya know, same old, same old. Ya gonna be around later."

"Don't know yet. Maybe."

"Ok, maybe I'll see you then." Spark says as he walks away.

This makes Jimmy curious. "They call you Sana?"

"Some people do. You gotta earn it, though."

"Cool. I'll keep that in mind. How do you know that guy?"

"He's just hung around here forever. I don't really know him." Osana tells Jimmy. The truth is she is well acquainted with Spark, a local drug dealer she buys from.

Spark, the only name most people know him by, got that name from the 'spark' he brings to people via the drugs he sells. He spends much of his time in the backstreets of the neighborhood. His presence is as much a part of the block as the graffiti-streaked walls and the worn-out stoops.

"Ok, but he called you Sana, right?"

"Maybe. Well, I gotta go, but it was nice talking to you – and thanks for the groceries."

"My pleasure. Don't mention it."

Jimmy leaves to walk back to his car until he realizes he has not asked for her phone number. He turns back quickly to catch before he gets too far. "Osana, wait!"

"What now?"

"I'd like to maybe call you once in a while, is it ok to get your number?"

Osana stands there thinking about it, finally agreeing.

"Thanks, I won't abuse it." Jimmy then rings her phone from his.

"You'd better not!" Osana says half laughingly.

"Now you got mine, too."

Osana begins walking back down the block and Jimmy watches her until she gets to her building. "I don't care what it takes I gotta see that ass without those stupid sweatpants on!" He returns to his car elated about the encounter.

███

Jimmy enters his apartment in a cheerful mode. Marie, observes him for a minute and says. "Well, someone's in a good mood today!"

"Who? Me?"

"Yeah, you. Did we hit the lottery or something?"

"Yeah, right! I wish."

"So, what happened?"

"Nothing happened, Marie." Jimmy protects his deception. "Can't I come home in a good mood?"

"You have to leave home to get in a good mood, I guess." Marie comes back with.

"I didn't say that. Don't put words in my mouth! Un-fuckin'-believable."

"Hey, the kids are in the other room, mister."

"Whatever."

Neither one of them says a word for quite a while. Jimmy is going through the mail and Marie is preparing food in the kitchen. She walks back to the dining area. "I only ask because you've been in a mood around here lately. I was curious what happened while you were out. Maybe you got good news you could share with your wife. I don't know."

"Well, if I was in a good mood, I ain't anymore."

"See! Everything I try to talk to you this happens!"

"Alright, sorry, let's forget it, ok?"

The baby's cries interrupt the spat as Marie heads to Jeannie's room. As she does, she tells Jimmy to call Bobby for lunch, and he does.

Talking Shit

O sana is on the phone with Bella, 'talking shit' and making plans to get high, when she comes out with. "Speaking about getting some cash, Bella, remember the garbage guy I was telling you about?"

"Who? That creepy guy... with the mustache?"

"Yeah, he's not that creepy. He was kind of nice when I talked to him."

"Talked to him? So, love is in the air, huh?"

"Eh, he's ok, not my type, but he did pay for all my groceries and my tab."

"When was this?"

"He showed up at the grocery store and we started talking."

"He lives around here?"

"No, I think he said Pelham Bay."

"Sana, that's far! Is he stalking you?"

"Don't get dramatic. He must have had something to do for work, maybe. He did have a wad of cash on him. I know that!"

"Oh! You got yourself a live one. So, it's love and money this time!"

"Shut up you! Who said anything about love?"

"Ha! Nobody. Just get what you can out of him. Guys like him want to be used, ya know."

"You're such a slut, Bella!"

"Look who's talking! How much cash have you taken from guys?"

"That's none of your business!" Osana says playfully. "Besides you don't have to be so straight up about it, like that."

"Girl, I've been getting high and doing shit like that with you forever, remember?"

"Yeah, I do. I guess I'm trying to be more lowkey nowadays. I promised I'd take it easy when I got back, but it looks like that went out the window already."

"Don't go getting soft on me now! They use us for enough shit."

"I won't. Don't worry. Maybe it's just I got the baby now." Osana considers.

"They know what the game is. We ain't doing nothing they don't know about, so it ain't like tricking them."

"It can get you some pretty good shit, that's for sure!"

"Yeah, if someone wants to spend their money on you, and you're upfront about it, it's ok." Bella suggests.

"I guess."

"I'm meeting a guy later. I can tell him to bring a friend if you want."

"Nah, I'm tired. I still got something to do around here."

"Really? Holding out on your old friend?"

"Why are you so stupid? Nothing like that! I mean work around the apartment."

"Ok, well let me know if you need a babysitter when you got something going on."

※

J immy spends the next few days going through his typical motions, waking up at 5:00 a.m., starting the coffee maker, brushing his teeth, shaving, and so on. By 5:30 a.m. he is in the kitchen pouring a bowl of cereal or grabbing a piece of fruit. Marie usually comes in at that point rubbing her eyes and joins him at the table. Jimmy is feeling indifferent towards her even as they exchange kisses and small talk.

As the clock inches toward 6:00 a.m., Jimmy finishes his food and grabs his work items. He gives Marie a quick hug and heads out the door. The drive to work is just as uneventful, the morning sun is rising, and he hits traffic in the usual spots. The routine is almost automatic as he moves through each step from years of repetition. Some people find comfort in such a routine, but Jimmy loathes it.

At work it is no different, he parks his car, punches in, and stops to see Mark for any special details. From there he joins Danny on the truck, and they set out to collect trash from their route. Lunch is at a local luncheonette where Danny tells the same old stories while Jimmy forces his food down. The afternoon is spent back on the truck finishing their route.

Their workday ends at 4:00 p.m., and Jimmy heads home. Sometimes Marie calls him to stop by the store to pick up ingredients for dinner. Back home, he, Marie, and the children share a pleasant evening. They eat dinner, watch their favorite television shows, take care of the children, and talk about their days.

Jimmy spends most of this time in his head, just barely paying attention. Especially lately looking forward to his next time with Osana. Thoughts of her fill his head at night before falling asleep.

T raveling their route a few days later Jimmy sees Osana walking down the block pushing her stroller, and he waves. She waves back with a big "Hey, how ya doing?"

Danny is surprised as he sees this through the rear-view mirrors but keeps the truck moving down the street. At the end of the day when Jimmy joins him in the cab, Danny brings it up. "Wow, so you and her are best buddies now?"

"Yeah, kind of. We met in the grocery store the other day."

"Wait, when the fuck were you at that grocery store?"

"On Saturday."

"Dude, don't tell me you came all the way back up here on your day off looking for her."

"What's it to you?!"

"Jimmy, are you going nuts? It's none of my business if you want to bang other women, but some crackhead?"

Jimmy takes offense to Danny's comment. "Maybe she's not a crackhead, just caught up in the bullshit of this fuckin' neighborhood. Ever think of that?"

"I'm just saying, dude. Think with your head, not your dick."

"She's a good-looking woman, that's all."

"She really is. I can't say I haven't noticed myself, but maybe for a BJ or something, but--"

"Why are we even talking about this?"

"You wouldn't leave Marie for something like that, would ya?"

"Who said anything about that? C'mon, Danny!"

They spend the rest of the ride to the yard in silence and are edgy with each other for the next couple of days. Jimmy regrets mentioning this to Danny for fear he may repeat it to people and Danny believes Jimmy is getting too carried away with this woman.

During a lunch break at work later in the week, Jimmy excuses himself to 'make a phone call' and walks about thirty feet away from Danny. He intends to call Osana but wonders if he should as he walks, not wanting to appear like a creep. He winds up leaning against a street light pole and calling her.

Osana answers the phone. "Hey, Jimmy."

"You knew it's me?"

"Sure, I saved your number."

"Nice! Thanks. I was just wondering how you were doing."

"Not too bad. I'd be better if my kitchen sink was working."

"What's the matter?"

"The water comes out, but only like dribbling." I told the super, but he takes forever to come by and look at shit.

"I can take a look at it if you want."

"Are you sure?"

"Of course. I'm pretty good with my hands."

"Well ok. I gotta get my daughter at three o'clock, but you can come by after that."

"That's perfect. I'll see you then."

Jimmy is ecstatic as he gets off the phone and walks back to join Danny in the luncheonette.

"I ate your fries." quips Danny.

"Of course, you did, ya fat fuck."

Danny laughs. "C'mon, back to work."

Jimmy spends the next few hours on the truck picturing how he's going to handle this next meeting with Osana. He figures it is best to play it cool, more laid back not to scare her off. Quitting time comes and Jimmy tells Danny to drop him off at the end of their route.

"Here? Where ya going, lad?"

"I got a side job to do."

"Would there be a pair of tits involved in this side job?"

"Fuck off. I just got to take care of something." Jimmy becomes defensive knowing Danny is aware of his intent but cannot resist the chance to meet Osana.

"Ok, whatever you say. See no evil..."

"I'm gonna borrow the toolbelt for tonight."

"Yeah, sure, go ahead."

The truck comes to a stop and Jimmy jumps out. He begins walking the opposite way from where he needs to go until

Danny has driven off. When he sees the truck make the right turn on Hunts Point Avenue, he reverses course and walks to Osana's building.

The Dance Lesson

Jimmy arrives, presses the intercom button, and waits for the door to buzz. As he does an elderly man appears from the back of the lobby and pushes the door slightly open. "It no work." he informs Jimmy.

"What? The buzzer?"

"Yeah, two days it no work." The man pushes the door wide open.

"Ah, thank you, my friend." Jimmy says as he passes and proceeds upstairs. After knocking on Osana's door she opens it. "I was gonna call you. The front door buzzer is broke."

"Yeah, I found out 'it no work'; some old guy told me." Jimmy says as a joke.

"Are you making fun of someone?" Osana asks lightheartedly.

"Me? No way. That's exactly what he told me!"

They chuckle a bit.

"Did you eat? I got some chicken out already." As she points to the kitchen.

"Wow, you gonna feed me, too. Cool."

As they eat the conversation involves stories about the neighborhood, their childhoods, and current events while finishing the bucket of chicken. Afterward, Jimmy checks her faucet and finds it is only a minor repair and takes care of it. He shows Osana it is working fine now.

"You're amazing." exclaims Osana.

"Hey, that was an easy one. The little strainer thing at the end of the faucet gets clogged with crap and stuff from our wonderful New York City drinking water.

"Crap? There's shit in my water?!"

Jimmy laughs. "Not real crap, I mean just small pieces of rust, like that."

"Whew, got 'cha. You deserve a beer!" Osana grabs two bottles of beer from the refrigerator and walks into the living room.

"Come, have a seat for a while" as she hands him a beer.

"I guess I can stay a while" and joins her. "I don't want to get anything dirty. I didn't get a chance to change out of my uniform."

"It's fine. You look ok to me."

Jimmy sits, looking around the living room he notices three cell phones on the coffee table and thinks it is odd. "You get a lot of calls?"

Osana turns and says "Not really. Why?"

Jimmy points to the phones. "Why do you have all those phones?" He has been around long enough to know this may be a sign of illegal activity.

"They're not all mine; friends forget them here sometimes." Osana tells him knowing they all belong to her, used for different schemes.

Jimmy doubts that but wants to believe her.

Osana puts on music and walks over to him. "Do you know how to dance?" she asks.

"Me? I can barely walk right."

"Ha, that's funny. I'll teach you. Stand up."

Jimmy stands up sheepishly. "I feel nervous, to be honest. I've never danced before. I don't want to make a fool out of myself."

Osana smiles. "Just trust me. You gotta let go and move with the music." She leads him to the center of the living room and gently guides him into a basic stance. Jimmy enjoys Osana's touch as she places her hands on his body. "The key is to make a connection and trust each other; just follow me."

Jimmy agrees as he tries to relax. As the soft, slow music plays Osana moves with a natural ease. She guides Jimmy through some basic steps, her movements are fluid, confident - and driving Jimmy wild. At first, Jimmy stumbles, his feet stepping on Osana's as he tries to sync with the rhythm. Osana is patient with him, guiding him with gentle corrections and reassuring words. "Listen to the music," she says in a soothing voice. "Feel the beat and let it guide you."

As the lesson progresses, Jimmy's nervousness begins to melt away. With Osana's calm instruction and the presence of the soft music, he starts to find his rhythm. He enjoys being so close to Osana, especially her breasts pressed against him. He is beginning to feel genuine relaxation, his mind becomes tranquil.

At one point, Jimmy looks up and catches Osana's eye. Her expression seems to be one of genuine joy, and in that moment, Jimmy feels this is not just a dance lesson but the making of a true bond with Osana.

As the music flows around them Jimmy loses himself in the dance and Osana. The world outside seems to fade, leaving just the two of them moving together in a harmonious embrace. When the music ends, Jimmy looks at Osana with fondness in his heart.

"Thank you, Osana." he says. "I didn't think I could move like that. It was fun."

Osana smiles. "You did great, Jimmy. I'll take you to the club one night."

"Sweet, I bet that'll be fun."

The two sit back down on the couch a little closer than before and finish their beers.

"I can't help but notice these paintings you have up. Where'd you get them?"

"You like them?"

"Yeah, they're beautiful, especially the one with all the trees. I feel relaxed just looking at it."

"I painted them."

"No, really?"

"Yeah, when I was younger, I used to paint a lot. Most of them got lost."

"Why'd you stop? You've got incredible talent."

"Ya know, things happen, get in the way. Maybe I'll get back to it one day if I ever get motivated again."

"You really should. I mean it. You motivated me today, maybe I can do the same for you sometime."

Osana looks at Jimmy knowing he is craving more of her.

Jimmy's strategy of being laid back comes back to him and he pauses for a moment. "It's getting late. I should start heading home."

"Someone waiting for you?"

"It's not that. I gotta get a cab, get home, change my clothes and work tomorrow. It takes a while." Jimmy says, averting attention from his obligations at home. He fears Osana may not be interested in him if he is married with children. He is still ignorant of this being of little consequence to her.

"Ok, well this was really nice. And thanks for the faucet."

"It's easy to help a beautiful woman."

"That's sweet." kissing him on the cheek.

Jimmy gets a spontaneous thought. "So, Osana, I can call out sick one day and maybe you can leave the baby with someone, and we go down to the city. How's that sound?"

"You mean like Downtown Manhattan?"

"Yeah, we can check out Central Park, a museum, and eat a couple hot dogs. It'll be fun."

"Ok. I haven't been down there to look around in a long time." Osana seems genuinely delighted. "When you want to go?"

"It's been a long time for me, too. Let's do it next Wednesday."

"All right, I'll ask my friend to watch the baby."

"Cool. I'm looking forward to it." Jimmy is quite pleased with the situation, and heads home.

The Big City

Jimmy spends time at home with Marie and the children carrying out the habits of everyday life. Yet, beneath the surface, Jimmy's thoughts are increasingly troubled. He walks around the apartment doing various small tasks and having short chats with his family, but his mind is not on any of those things. He decides to relax by watching television. Everyone else is occupied in other parts of the apartment. Looking down at his phone he sees a new message notification. Jimmy opens the message excitedly.

It is a simple "Hi, how are you?" from Osana. To Jimmy, those four words are bursting with possibilities. He hesitates before responding, but the words flow easily when he does. Jimmy is amazed at how effortless the conversation is with Osana; he usually struggles to maintain even a brief exchange with people. But their talks are filled with light banter and a shared sense of humor Jimmy finds charming.

As messages go back and forth, Jimmy glances at the family photographs hanging on the wall, a visual timeline of his years with Marie. All the memories and smiles frozen in time unexpectedly seem meaningless to him. The thrill of the conversation with Osana stirs something in Jimmy, he feels alive, the adventure of the unknown. He wonders what it would be like to spend more time with her. Osana tells him her baby is getting restless, so she needs to go.

As the texts end, Marie calls out to him from the other room. "I'm running to the supermarket, you gonna be here?"

"Yeah, I'm just hanging out." Jimmy answers over his shoulder.

"Ok, see you in a bit." With that Marie walks out of the door.

Jimmy does his best to watch the children, but he cannot stop his mind from wandering back to his phone. He envisions leaving everything to be with Osana. As days pass, he becomes less focused on his own family as the attraction to Osana grows. He knows leaving will not be easy but believes Osana has awakened the part of him that has been absent his whole life.

W ednesday comes and Osana brushes out her long black hair and applies what little makeup she uses to brighten up her face. Instead of her usual jeans and t-shirt, she opts for a tighter-fitting dress to enhance her curvy body with cleavage to intensify Jimmy's attentiveness. Jimmy has a dilemma, however. He cannot dress too far out of the norm because Marie thinks he is going to work. Planning to change into a nicer shirt and shoes he stashes them in the car ahead of time.

Jimmy finally arrives at Osana's as scheduled and immediately notices Osana's appearance. "Wow, you look so amazing!"

"Gee, thank you, Jimmy. It's just a casual dress, nothing special."

"Yeah, you should wear it all the time." Jimmy is amazed at getting his first good look at what her body is shaped like. Her top and bottom are more pronounced than he has imagined.

"That'd get a little boring after a while!" Osana laughs. "Here, can you take Amy?"

Jimmy takes Amy and her stroller out into the hallway while Osana locks the door. They drop Amy off at Bella's, then get a livery cab to the subway. Jimmy tells Osana the trip will be easier by train rather than bringing the car into Manhattan, but, in truth, he does not want to pay the tolls or parking.

During the subway ride, they get to know each other better and make fun of some of the other riders. At one point they hold hands. Jimmy is excited about this but is also concerned someone he knows might see them.

Jimmy tracks the stops on the map in the subway car to make sure he knows where to get off, not to look like he doesn't know his way around, and sees their stop is next. "Ok, here we go! Let's stand up. The doors are gonna open on that side." Jimmy instructs.

Jimmy and Osana push their way through the crowded subway car, as the doors open, they step off and proceed up the stairs to street level. It is a beautiful spring morning. The sun is shining through the towering skyscrapers, casting a golden glow over the bustling streets. The city is alive with the promise of a perfect day, and so is Jimmy. Their first stop is Central Park. The air is fragrant with blooming flowers and the sound of conversations and laughter fills the paths. Osana and Jimmy wander hand in hand, the vibrant colors of the season surrounding them. New blossoms paint the trees in soft pinks and whites, and the scent of new growth is everywhere.

Jimmy notices a group of children playing in one of the fields and turns to Osana. "Hey, maybe we should have brought a frisbee. We could have played over there."

Osana giggles. "Maybe next time! I'm not dressed for that today!"

"I see. What are you dressed for?"

"Why don't you try and find out?"

Jimmy thinks of just how eager he is to do that.

They continue down the winding paths, stopping at a vendor cart to buy cups of coffee. With those in hand, they find a bench overlooking the lake. Rowboats glide across the water, couples laugh and splash as they paddle in sync.

"Can you believe this is in the middle of a huge city?" Jimmy asks, taking a sip of his coffee.

"I know, it's amazing. What was here before?" Osana replies.

"What do you mean?" Jimmy asks confoundedly.

"Did they knock a lot of stuff down to plant all this?"

Jimmy holds in his amusement as he realizes how she thinks the park came about. "No, this park, this nature was here first. They built the city around it. I think they changed it a little, but it was here before the city."

"Oh, I get it now." Osana looks around. "I'm embarrassed to say, but I was never in here."

Jimmy grins. "Well, to tell you the truth, neither have I!"

They laugh as they finish their coffees. And start strolling again.

"What do you love most about this place?" Osana asks, looking at Jimmy.

"Being here with you." he responds bashfully.

Osana leans over and kisses him on the cheek. "Thank you, Jimmy. That's nice to say."

"I'm not just saying it, I really mean it. I feel different around you."

From the park, they make their way, arm in arm, to the Metropolitan Museum of Art. Jimmy thinks this should interest the painter in Osana. As they wander the collections the conversation continues to flow.

By noon, hunger leads them to a deli where they enjoy pastrami sandwiches and share a pickle or two. The place is bustling with locals and has a charm that perfectly encapsulates the city's essence. Jimmy is happy to see that Osana is truly enjoying their excursion.

As the afternoon unfolds, they venture down the avenues, to admire the high-end storefronts. Osana makes them stop to see the street performers, adding a touch of whimsy to the scene. She is mesmerized by a street artist who is painting vibrant portraits. Jimmy suggests she sit for one and she does. The artist's rendition of her captures her with exaggerated features and playful flair.

It is getting later in the afternoon by now. Jimmy needs to get home in time to maintain the appearance of a normal workday.

"Have you had enough of the city yet?" Jimmy probes.

"I think so. This was a good idea, Jimmy. I really enjoyed it."

"That makes me happy, Osana. Let's start walking to the subway."

The subway ride home has less conversation since they are tired from walking so much. Jimmy feels a bond as Osana rests her head on his shoulder for most of the ride. When Jimmy arrives home, only slightly later than usual, Marie does not seem to show any signs of suspicion.

❦❦❦

J immy lies in bed, his mind a whirlwind of thoughts, each one pulling him in a different direction. Two women, two paths, and an uncertain future. The cool sheets feel strangely comforting against his skin, but the decision presses on him.

First, there is Marie, his wife, and the mother of his children. Their relationship is comfortable, but he cannot declare he is in love with her. He admits she is a good mother and keeps their lives running well. It is not a bad marriage, but not fulfilling. It seems the two of them just go through the motions, never truly engaging as he thinks they should. He suspects Marie feels the same way but would never admit it. She calls him 'babe' and 'honey' frequently and holds his hand whenever they walk together, but perceives her mind is elsewhere.

Osana, on the other hand, is a burst of energy, unpredictable and vibrant. He sees a relationship with her being filled with passion and a love for life. Osana challenges him in ways he never imagined, pushing him to confront his fears and desires. Her presence is like a storm—intense and invigorating, but also capable of leaving damage in its wake.

Jimmy fixes his pillow and blanket. He is unsure if leaving all he built behind and going with Osana is the right choice. He suspects it is, but the fear of making a mistake looms large. But he is eager to find a path that will bring him happiness. He closes his eyes and imagines a life with each of them.

The clock on the nightstand ticks away, like an audible reminder of the choice he faces. He has faith the decision will come down to what is right in his heart, not logically. He turns to his side and lets the darkness wrap around him.

The Emergency Room

"That was another great day!" Danny exclaims as they head back to the depot.

"Hey, ya know what, just drop me off here." Jimmy asks.

"Here? What are you up to now?"

"Danny, just drop me off. I gotta cool my head for a while."

Hesitantly Danny pulls the truck over to the curb; Jimmy jumps out. "Thanks. I'll see you tomorrow."

"If that's what you want. Be careful around here, lad. Make sure you get out by dark." Danny warns.

Jimmy tells him he'll be fine, closes the truck door, and walks away moodily. After walking for a while, he passes a small neighborhood bar and supposes he will stop in for a beer, maybe two. He enters and sits on a stool. "Gimme whatever you got on draft." he tells the bartender.

Jimmy surveys the place as he drinks. The bar is sparsely occupied with ragged-looking denizens of the battered area. He feels like he belongs with the rest of these lost souls, though.

As he gestures to the bartender to bring him his fourth beer the front door opens filling the bar with the last minutes of daylight. Jimmy pivots his head to see who is coming in and sees it's Osana. She is dressed differently, with her hair pulled back in a ponytail and wearing a skimpy dress that shows off her full figure.

"Osana?" The words spew out of his mouth like an involuntary reflex.

"Oh hey, Jimmy! Wow, it's weird seeing you here." Osana feels embarrassed running into Jimmy but does not let on.

"Yeah, I just stopped in for a beer after work."

"One beer?" Osana questions since it is obvious Jimmy has had quite a few.

"Yeah, ya know, one leads thing to another, right?"

"We'll see about that! So, you gonna buy me a drink?"

"Of course!" Jimmy exclaims and calls the bartender over. Osana orders a double bourbon, neat.

"Wow," says Jimmy. "That's a pretty potent drink!"

"Well, I don't like to waste time." Osana says teasingly.

"Cool, I'm glad to hear that. I'm kind of surprised to see you here, though."

"Why's that?"

"I don't know. It doesn't seem like your kind of place." Jimmy says, looking her scant outfit up and down; too inexperienced to grasp why she is dressed in such a way.

"Sometimes I just drop the baby off for a while and come here to have a drink, that's all." Osana doesn't tell him the truth. She was hoping to turn a couple tricks to pick up some extra money. "So, thanks for the trip to the city. I enjoyed it, Jimmy."

"Me, too. Thank you for coming."

Jimmy notices she keeps looking past him at something or someone and asks her about it. "Is someone you know back there?"

"No, why?"

"I don't know, you keep looking over my shoulder."

"No, nobody. Hey, we seem to be meeting all the time now, huh?" Osana hastily changes the subject.

They chuckle a bit. They sit and drink and talk for some time. Jimmy tries to hide the fact his cell phone is ringing every few minutes. Osana has dealt with various married men and is well aware it is his wife calling him; she ribs him about it.

"Is that your mother calling?" With a smile on her face.

"Ha! Yeah, it's my mother." Jimmy replies sarcastically.

"Maybe you should get home then?"

Jimmy wavers, choosing between his options. He could stay with the woman he's been waiting for or go home and minimize the hassle he faces. Somehow the rational part of his brain kicks in and decides to go home. "Well, nothing like that, but I do have to get to work early tomorrow, so I guess I'd better call it a night."

"That's too bad, I thought we were just getting to know each other."

"It doesn't have to be the last time. What are you doing Friday night?"

"I think I could be available. What are you thinking?" Osana says coyly.

"We can go get something to eat and hang out."

"Ok, sounds like a plan. I'm gonna have to get a babysitter, though. I'll see if I have enough cash for that." Osana says, testing him.

"How much is that?"

"Oh no, I'm not asking for anything, just thinking out loud." She feigns to be shy about it.

"Hey, if I want to take you out, I don't mind paying for it."

That's the perfect response to Osana's ears. She's established it's easy to get Jimmy to open his wallet. "Well... I guess it's ok."

"Great. I'll come get you on Friday at 7:00 p.m."

Osana says she's excited and kisses Jimmy on the cheek intensifying his yearning for her – just as she intended.

"Are you heading home, too?" Jimmy asks.

"Um, no, not right now. I'll just finish this drink first. It's ok you can go ahead. I'll be ok."

Jimmy walks unstably out of the bar wishing he could have stayed.

✾✾✾

J immy arrives at his apartment and stands at the front door, key in hand. He is dreading the reception he is going to receive when he walks in, but Marie is nowhere to be found when he does. He steps further in and finds her in their bedroom with Jeannie, who is laid out on the bed. Jimmy asks, "Is she ok?"

Marie answers with tears in his eyes "I don't know, Jimmy. What should we do?"

Jimmy is coming down from his intoxicated state and is having trouble considering their next actions. "Well, what happened?"

"I went to feed her a little while ago and she wouldn't eat and looked pale; just kind of laying in her crib." They decide to take her to the emergency room, so they get the baby ready and head down to the car.

Jimmy confesses to Marie he had 'a few drinks,' so she would have to drive. Her annoyance at this is outweighed by the need to get to the hospital, so she acquiesces. Jimmy sits in the back with Jeannie trying to keep her as comfortable as possible.

When they arrive at the emergency room, the waiting area is surprisingly empty. Jimmy is carrying Jeannie, who has be-gun to quiet down, though her distress is still evident. Marie approaches the reception desk, her voice steady but strained as she explains their situation.

The triage nurse, a kind-faced woman named Becky, quickly assesses Jeannie's condition and leads them to an exam room in the back. Within moments, a pediatrician named Dr. Watson enters, his calm demeanor provides a mea-sure of reassurance. Marie tells the doctor how Jeannie is behaving and a host of information from her primary doctor.

Dr. Watson listens attentively. "Let's have a look." he says gently.

Jeannie, still a bit irritable, is placed on the examination table, and Dr. Watson begins his assessment. After a thorough examination and a few tests, Dr. Watson talks with Marie and Jimmy. "I can understand what you have been going through, it must be quite distressing. But truthfully, there is not much we can do for her tonight, except keep her here to make sure she's comfortable."

Jimmy speaks up timidly. "Doctor, I think we appreciate what you're saying, but isn't that something we can do at home? I'm just thinking of the insurance and, you know..."

Marie gestures to Jimmy to be quiet.

"I understand, Mr. Rizzo. It is possible as long as you follow some recommendations until you can get her to her primary doctor. I truly wish there was more we could do for her, but I doubt there's anything to worry about tonight."

Marie and Jimmy are exhausted but grateful. The stress of the evening begins to wane as they gather Jeannie and her things and travel home. In the car, Marie comments she wishes someone could tell them exactly what is going on with Jeannie so they could come to some resolution.

"I know. But you're doing the right thing. The doctors know what they're doing." Jimmy tells her. Marie wipes a tear from her eye, but his saying 'you're doing the right thing' strikes her as strange.

Back at home, Marie gets Jeannie to eat this time. Jimmy reheats some food for Marie and him and everyone beds down for the night. Jimmy is relieved nothing was asked about his prior whereabouts.

T he next morning Jimmy awakens to find Marie next to Jeannie's crib. "Have you been up all night? he asks, rubbing the sleep from his eyes.

"Pretty much. I slept for a bit, but I just wanted to make sure she was ok."

"Any more issues during the night?"

"No, no just the usual feeding and diaper changes."

"That's good. Do you think we can take her to the doctor today?

"I'm going to call as soon as the office opens at 9:00 a.m. They should take her right away." Marie says, hoping she is right.

"I'll call out sick to go with you." Jimmy proposes, thinking this is what Marie is waiting for.

Marie is pleased but also surprised by his offer. "You don't have to. I can get there. Go to work."

"No, Marie, I want to go. It's fine."

Marie looks at Jimmy with gratitude in her eyes and nods in agreement. At 9:00 a.m. sharp Marie dials the phone as she said and talks the doctor's assistant into bringing Jeannie in that morning.

The ride to the doctor's office is a quiet one. Jimmy's mind is mostly on Osana, thinking he is missing an opportunity to see her again by calling out sick. Marie is mentally reviewing the questions she is going to ask the doctor.

As they arrive at the office, they find the waiting room full of people and more than a few babies crying. Jimmy takes a seat holding Jeannie while Marie goes up to the reception window.

"Oh yes, Mrs. Rizzo. You can bring Jeannie right in. The doctor will see you." the receptionist informs her.

They enter the examination room, where Jeannie's cardiologist, Dr. Patel, greets them with a warm smile. "So, I hear you guys brought her to the emergency room last night?"

"Yes, doctor. She wasn't doing well, and Jimmy and me got panicky. I'm sorry."

"Sorry? What are you sorry about? You're worried about your daughter. Let's take a look at this beautiful little girl." he says, examining Jeannie with a gentle touch.

After his examination, Dr. Patel turns to the parents. "Jeannie is doing well, but we need to start her on medication to help support her heart. We must monitor her condition closely."

"What will the medication do?" Marie asks.

Dr. Patel explains how the prescriptions would help Jeannie's heart pump more efficiently. He outlines the dosages and side effects, taking his time to ensure they understand everything. "You're doing a great job as parents," he reassures them. "With the right care, Jeannie has every chance to thrive."

After the appointment, the couple goes directly to a nearby pharmacy and picks up the medications. That evening they spent time figuring out a routine to carefully administer them. Since Marie is home most of the time, she will do the overnight and daytime rounds and Jimmy is scheduled to take care of this when he is home in the evenings. However, after a few times of him failing to follow the plan Marie takes over his hours, too.

The same thoughts persist in Jimmy's head. He needs to figure out how he is going to meet up with Osana on Friday when it comes to him. He will tell Marie that he needs to go out for a co-worker's bachelor's party. So far, Marie has no real reason to disbelieve him but questions him.

"So, who are these guys you're going with?"

"Guys from work, no one you ever met."

"Well, where's the party going to be? Around here?"

"Why? You plan on showing up?"

"I'm just asking. Can't I ask a question?"

"Yeah, you're right. I don't know the place. I think it's in Yonkers or something."

"Oh. Are we invited to the wedding?"

"I don't think so. I didn't get anything yet. Maybe tonight he'll tell me."

"They don't send out invitations? What kind of people are they?"

"Marie, gimme me a break. When I find out I will tell you."

When he gets home from work on Friday, he eats dinner hurriedly and begins preparing for his night out. He opts for his black suede loafers, a dress shirt, and his good slacks. He also spends an odd amount of time on his hair. Once ready, he paces around the apartment glancing at the clock frequently. At one point Marie asks why he keeps checking himself out in the mirror. Jimmy ignores the question.

The time to leave comes and Jimmy walks into the living room where Marie is watching television. "Ok, I'm gonna go now."

"Be careful and don't drink too much. Take a cab home if you have to. Don't drive."

"Don't worry I won't. Although these things can get pretty crazy sometimes." Jimmy adds, faking a laugh.

"Just don't do anything stupid, that's all."

"Yes, dear," Jimmy says sarcastically.

The Vape Pen

Jimmy jumps in his car and makes his way to Osana's. "Oh shit, I should bring something, shouldn't I?" After running through different possibilities in his mind, he decides to bring one single rose and stops to buy one on the way.

As he drives, he mentally reviews the plan for the evening. First, dinner at a relaxed Italian restaurant he knows in the Castle Hill section. It is not far from Osana's apartment, but far enough from where he lives. After dinner he figures they will go back to her place, so he does not think of any arrangements after the restaurant.

He pulls up to Osana's building and fixes his clothes after stepping out of the car. He is happy to see the street is quiet, so he will not be seen. Jimmy's heart is palpitating as he arrives at her apartment door.

He knocks and after a moment the door swings open, and there stands Osana. She is dressed in a short, simple green dress that is somewhat more revealing than Jimmy is comfortable with, particularly on top. But the color does bring out her eyes and makes her smile even brighter. Her hair is pulled back in soft waves, and she has a subtle but enchanting fragrance.

"Hi, Jimmy!" Osana greets him with a warm smile, her eyes sparkling. "I'm so glad to see you."

Jimmy stands there wondering if he should lean in for a kiss, but Osana beats him to it. "Hi, Osana. You look incredible. And that dress... I'm probably gonna have to fight some guys off tonight." Jimmy says.

"Oh, stop. It's just a plain dress."

"That dress ain't plain, and you certainly aren't. You ready to go?"

"I dropped the baby off at my friend's already, so I'm free as a bird!" she replies with an excited nod. "Let me just grab my purse."

As Osana gathers her purse and a light sweater, Jimmy feels there is something about her making him feel at ease. His mind slows down, and his spirit rises around her.

When they get to Jimmy's car, he opens the door for her, a gesture she surely appreciates; he guesses no one has ever done this for her. Osana slides into the passenger seat, adjusting her dress as she does.

The drive to the restaurant is filled with relaxed conversation. They talk about everything from the weather to their favorite foods. Osana's laughter is like music to Jimmy's ears. He finds himself joking and sharing stories more freely than he anticipated.

"So, how 'bout you, Osana? Any funny stories from when you were a kid?" Jimmy asks harmlessly, not recognizing they have grown up in two very different worlds. This will become apparent to him as they get to know each other better.

"Oh, ya know, just the usual little kid stuff. Are we almost there yet? I'm getting hungry." Osana asks as she tries to quell some of the memories Jimmy stirred with his question.

"Yeah, it's only a few more blocks."

At the restaurant, they are led to a cozy table by the window. The restaurant is intimate, with dim lighting and soft music playing in the background. They order a selection of dishes to share, and the conversation continues without missing a beat.

Osana has a way of drawing Jimmy out, making him feel like he is the most interesting person in the world. It is as though they are uncovering a new layer of connection with each passing minute. After dessert and coffee, they get ready for the rest of the night. As they walk back to the car, Jimmy asks what she would like to do.

"I know a club near here we can go to."

"Ok, sure. Your wish is my command, my lady!" Jimmy consents happily.

Osana laughs.

After some directions from Osana, she points out they have arrived at the club. As they drive by, the outside is not what Jimmy expects. It appears to be more of an unauthorized after-hours spot, than a legal establishment. It has what looks like the overhead signage from a previous store and the windows are blacked out. There is only one small LED sign flashing 'OPEN' showing any sign of an active business. But it is closer to Hunts Point, which makes Jimmy think they still may end up at her apartment.

Jimmy finds a parking space down the block and as they walk to the club Osana asks if Jimmy would mind if she vaped.

"No, of course not. Go for it." Jimmy promptly consents.

"Thanks." Osana proceeds to take a vape pen out of her purse.

"I heard those are good to quit smoking."

Osana giggles. "Maybe I should have said, this ain't nicotine, Jimmy."

It takes Jimmy a couple of seconds to process her statement but realizes what she is suggesting. "Oh, I got 'cha. It's pot, right?" Jimmy is blindsided with having to face drug use on this date, and worries about the legalities, but wants to please Osana.

"Weed, yeah, it's that ok?"

"Sure, no big deal." Jimmy plays it cool, uneasy with the position he has been put in.

"You want to try it?" Osana holds the vape pen out hoping to tempt him.

Jimmy cautiously agrees. "Why not, right?"

Osana takes a toke off the pen first and hands it to Jimmy. He takes a toke, his eyes wide with curiosity. It is smoother than he expects, carrying a faint minty flavor. He exhales slowly as Osana watches with anticipation and amusement.

"Wow, it kind of tickles my throat. I didn't expect it to be like this."

Osana grins "Yeah, it's pretty chill."

Jimmy takes another, deeper toke, and immediately feels warmer, and the colors and lights around him appear more vibrant. Without realizing he lets out a small chuckle.

Osana nods knowingly. "That's the high kicking in, you're gonna feel relaxed."

Jimmy feels his muscles unwind from the pressure he has been holding in for years. "Whoa," he says, letting out a long sigh. "I feel like I'm floating."

"I'm glad you're enjoying it."

"Yeah, but should we be doing it out in the open like this?"

"Nobody's around. I guess we're ready to get inside, anyway." Osana says as she takes him by the arm.

The two proceed to enter the club and take seats at a small table. They order drinks and talk some more. Jimmy is very tranquil as he glances around the club through his altered eyes. "This is amazing... you're amazing, Osana." He says with a smile. Osana simply smiles back.

As Osana chats with a woman at a nearby table she can tell Jimmy is lost in his thoughts. He looks engrossed in simple things like the way the lights played on the ceiling or the rhythm of the music.

Jimmy realizes he is laughing often, even at the smallest things. "This is definitely not what I was expecting," he tells Osana when she sits back down with him.

"It's all about the feeling," Osana says. "I'm glad you're having a good time."

"Can I ask you something, babe?"

"Sure, anything."

"Is a guy who leaves his sick kid at home to go out partying a scumbag?"

"What kind of question is that?!" Osana is surprised by the subject.

"I don't know. Just something that ran through my head."

"Forget it, Jimmy. Don't ruin the night. Finish your drink." Osana aims to bring his mind back to the present. Thinking of his family is the last thing she wants Jimmy to focus on tonight.

They sit for a while more, have another drink, and talk amongst themselves and people nearby. As time goes on, Jimmy finds himself feeling very intoxicated, and, as much as he hates to admit it, he needs to get home. Thinking of a reasonable excuse he comes out with. "Well, I gotta take care of some shit in the morning, so I think I'd better drop you off."

"Really? I thought we were just getting started."

"I know. I hate to be the party pooper, but ya know..."

As Osana says goodbye to a few friends she hands money to one of them and they slip something back to her. Jimmy sees this but is too high to attach any significance to it.

In the car, Jimmy is so focused on driving in his condition there is little conversation during the trip to Osana's. He is able to park and walk her back up to the apartment, though.

As they stand in her doorway Jimmy has a sense of serenity, even though the night did not go exactly as planned. "I had a wonderful time tonight," his voice is sincere. "I hope you did too."

Osana looks at him with a smile. "I had an amazing time, Jimmy. Thank you."

They stand there for a moment, looking at each other. Jimmy has a surge of courage to go in for a passionate kiss and pulls her into him roughly. The two kiss heatedly for a couple of minutes in her doorway before Osana pulls away.

"I'm sorry, Osana. I couldn't help—"

"There's nothing to be sorry for. Except you leaving now." Osana says suggestively.

"I'm sorry, we'll have to get together again real soon."

Osana's grins as she gives his hand a gentle squeeze. "I'd love to."

"Maybe I'll handle vaping better next time." They laugh.

Osana goes into her bag and pulls the vape pen out. "Here you can take this one."

"Oh no, that's ok. I don't need it." Assorted scenarios run through his head from the police finding it during a traffic stop to Marie discovering it in his pocket.

"Go ahead. Just hold onto it. You never know you might need a hit once in a while."

"I guess it can't hurt." Jimmy says as he takes the pen out of her hand and puts it in his pocket. "Good night, Osana. Thank you."

Jimmy gets back to his car and starts driving, hoping he will not get pulled over by the police. It is not effortless for him to drive, but he makes it home without incident. As he enters his apartment, he is pleased to find everyone sleeping.

The Dinner Date

Jimmy wakes up later than usual, and the house is buzzing with warm, cozy energy. Sunlight streams through the bedroom window. He walks into the kitchen to find Marie whipping up a batch of chocolate chip pancakes for their son. The table is already set and there are plates of fresh fruit at each seat.

In the living room, Bobby is with Jeannie in her bouncy chair, their laughter echoes through the house as they play with their favorite toys.

"Daddy, look at my castle!" Bobby calls out, his face lit with pride as he shows off a towering construction made from colorful blocks.

"That's amazing!" Jimmy says back, as Marie places pancakes in front of him. "Can I come see it when I'm done with breakfast?"

"Sure! I'm a knight and Jeannie is the queen,"

"Everything looks wonderful. Thanks for making breakfast." Jimmy tells Marie.

Marie leans over and gives him a quick peck on the cheek. "Anything for you and the kids," Marie says, returning his smile. "It's nice to have a day like this—just us."

They gather around the table, and as they eat Bobby regales them with tales of his kindergarten class, as Marie feeds Jeannie.

As Jimmy observes these doings in front of him it produces a chaotic reaction within him. This is the life he believes he has been wanting but never expected it to happen at home. He soon persuades himself this is a one-time occurrence, and he should not put any faith in it.

After breakfast, Marie suggests a family outing at the local park. Bobby cheers at the idea, and Marie packs up the baby's items, some drinks, and snacks before heading out. At the park, Jimmy lays out the blanket and Marie unpacks the food.

"Mommy, can I help." Bobby asks.

"Of course you can, I would love that. Can you take the sandwiches out and put them here?" Marie instructs him with a smile. "This reminds me of the picnics when I was a kid." Marie mentions.

"You had picnics, too?" Bobby is captivated.

"Oh sure, we did! My parents would take us, and my father would come up with silly games for us to play."

"Your father? Play games? I don't believe it." Jimmy chimes in.

"He sure did. Sometimes he would hide some coins around and we'd have to go find them, like a treasure hunt."

Bobby turns to Jimmy. "Can we do that, daddy? I want to find some coins."

"Sure, my boy. You wait here and I'll go hide some and promise you won't look!"

Jimmy complies and walks around the park hiding his pocket change next to trees and playground equipment. He leads Bobby around until all of it is found before heading back to the blanket.

"Mommy, look at all the money I have!" Bobby is so excited.

"Wow, you're rich now. So, are you guys ready to eat?

"Can we go on the swings first, mommy? We didn't do any of that stuff yet?"

"Ok, you guys have fun."

When Jimmy and Bobby return later, they dig into their sandwiches while Marie pays attention to Jeannie. After their picnic, as they're packing up Marie turns to Jimmy. "The simple things make up the best memories, don't they?"

"I guess." Jimmy says indifferently.

Marie looks at him with a bewildered look on her face.

B ack at the apartment, Marie bathes the children while Jimmy puts away the picnic gear. As things wind down and the kids are taking naps, Jimmy and Marie find themselves sitting on the couch alone.

"Today was perfect," Marie says softly.

"Yeah, it was fun," Jimmy agrees. He sits quietly for a few minutes, looking at Marie he feels a touch of guilt. He thinks he should do something special for her, too. So, he comes up with a suggestion. "Hey Marie, why don't we go to dinner tonight?"

"Dinner? Wow, what made you think of that?"

"I don't know. We haven't been anywhere in forever, so I thought maybe dinner at a nice restaurant would break things up."

"With the kids?"

"Nope, just me and you. Can you get one of your friends to babysit on short notice?"

"Yeah, I think Gina can be available." Marie pauses. "I'll have to give her instructions to take care of Jeannie."

"She can handle it. Anyway, we'll have our phones with us, so she can call if anything happens, and we won't go too far. C'mon, we'll get all dolled up and hit the town!" Jimmy insists.

"Oh, I can't wait! It's been so long. Thank you for thinking of this." Marie leans over and gives Jimmy a big kiss on the cheek.

"Hey, happy wife, happy life, right?"

They laugh and hug each other.

"You know what else they say?" Jimmy asks.

"No, why don't you tell me." Marie says, expecting another joke.

"No wife, no strife!"

Marie slaps him on the arm playfully.

Jimmy is genuinely in a better mood this evening, but his mind is still longing for his next meeting with Osana.

*   *   *

J immy is dressed in a sharp, tan suit, while Marie is in a attractive, but dated blue dress. They haven't worn these outfits since the last wedding they attended before the children were born. Jimmy makes sure to comment on how beautiful Marie looks and Marie compliments him.

The night is off to a great start as they drive to the restaurant on Arthur Avenue. They tell funny stories about when they first met and were getting to know each other. Jimmy opens the car door and takes her hand as she steps out into the evening air.

Inside the restaurant, the ambiance is warm and inviting, with low romantic lighting and soft instrumental music playing. The maître d' leads them to their table, which is adorned with a white tablecloth and flickering candles. Marie settles in, looking around with a pleased smile.

"I've heard great things about this place," Jimmy says sitting across from her. "They're known for their fish dishes and excellent wine."

The evening is unfolding delightfully. They enjoy their delicate appetizers, and especially savor their main courses; each has a glass of wine or two to complement the flavors. As they finish dessert, Jimmy is caught up in the moment and takes Marie's hand and tells her. "Life gets so busy, and sometimes we forget to just be with each other. I want to make sure we have nights like this once in a while."

Marie's eyes softened, and she gives his hand a gentle squeeze. "I feel the same way. Let's not forget to enjoy the simple moments."

Leaving the restaurant, Jimmy wraps his arm around Marie, pulling her close. They walk back to the car, the night air cool and refreshing.

"Thank you for tonight," Marie says as they drive home. "It was perfect."

Jimmy smiles. "It was my pleasure, but who said the night is over?"

Marie giggles "Oh stop it! Behave yourself."

Arriving home, they are met at the door by Gina; she and Marie begin talking. Jimmy heads for the bedroom to undress.

"How did it go, Gina?"

"Everything was fine. They ate, Jeannie was fine all night, no issues. They're sound asleep now. Bobby was trying to stay awake for you guys but couldn't hold out anymore."

Marie giggles. "He's not used to us being out, I guess."

"You guys should do this more often. I don't mind watching them."

"Thanks, Gina. Maybe we will. Well, it's late and I'd better let you go." Marie tries handing Gina money, but she refuses and says good night.

Marie checks on the children then heads for their bedroom. "Gina's really nice. She says we should go out more often, too." She waits for a response but does not get one. "Jimmy?... Jimmy?" She realizes he has already fallen asleep.

"Well, so much for behaving yourself, huh." She, in turn, undresses and goes to sleep.

Isn't This Illegal?

Marie is up well before Jimmy the next morning. She comes up from the laundry room and begins putting the clean clothes back in their proper drawers. She goes about her tasks as quietly as possible. Putting the children's clothes back is as uneventful as usual.

It comes time to put Jimmy's clothes away. His socks are last to be placed because they are in the bottom drawer, Marie needs to kneel to do this. As she pushes some of the socks to the side, she hears something hard scrape against the bottom. She pushes more socks out of the way and discovers a vape pen. She reads the side, and it is marked 'THC.' She stares at it, her mind is struggling to understand where it came from. The bewilderment soon turns to anger. "Jimmy! What the hell is this? Jimmy!"

Jimmy wakes up shaking his head not sure what is happening. "What? What happened?" he says trying to wake up.

Marie holding the pen up. "This! Where did this come from?"

"Where did what come from? Jimmy questions as he sits up in bed. He looks towards Marie, and he sees the vape pen in her hand. 'Oh fuck!' he thinks to himself. He needs to come up with a story quickly. "Oh, that? I found it on my route. I kept it as a joke."

"A marijuana pen is not a joke! You know how I hate drugs."

"Marijuana? I thought it was one of those nicotine things."

"You're full of shit, Jimmy. It says 'THC' right on the side. Are you doing drugs now?"

"No, what are you kidding?" Jimmy is struggling for words; he has guilt etched on his face. He tries to grab the pen, but Marie pulls away.

"You're not getting this. What do you want it for?"

"I messed up, I know. I'm sorry. I'll throw it away. I promise."

Marie shakes her head, tears welling up in her eyes. "It's not just about the vape pen, Jimmy. You're lying to me; I don't know what's going on. You're acting very strange lately."

"I used it once, that's all, I swear."

"Then you knew what it was! Where'd you get it from? Isn't this illegal?"

"I found it on my route, really. I just wanted to try it."

Marie faces distorts with disgust. "God knows who had their mouth on this thing! Did you think of that?"

"I did kind of wipe it off." Jimmy says uneasily.

Marie wants to believe him about the vape but questions what is going on. "I need to think," she says, her voice barely above a whisper. "You're making me worry and I have enough on my mind."

"Marie, c'mon, didn't we have a great time last night?"

"Yeah, probably because you're guilty about something. Is that it?" Marie leaves the room clutching the vape pen. Jimmy hears her go out into the hallway and gathers she is going to throw it down the garbage chute. He knows looking for it down in the basement will be useless. He can always get another one from Osana regardless.

"Tell me what's going on?" Marie shouts as she storms back into the bedroom.

"You know what then, Marie, you want time to think? I'll give you time to think – by yourself." Jimmy gets dressed hurriedly and storms out of the apartment.

❦

Jimmy drives around for quite a while finally deciding to go see Osana and gives her a call. "Good morning, babe. How ya doing?"

Osana awakened by the call is somewhat confused talking to him at first. "Oh, hey Jimmy. What's up?"

"Not much, I just thought I could bring you some coffee and breakfast and maybe the baby needs something."

"Cool, that'd be nice." She gives him what she would like and a couple of things the baby needs. Jimmy happily stops at a diner and a couple of stores to get everything.

He makes it to her place at last and they sit in the kitchen area and eat together, with Amy in her highchair having her cereal.

The three of them wind up in the living room with Amy in her bouncy seat and Jimmy and Osana finishing their coffees on the couch. Jimmy dozes off as the television news drones on, waking up late in the afternoon.

"Osana, wow, I'm so sorry. I didn't mean to—"

Osana laughs. "That's ok. You must have been tired."

"Yeah, I guess I am. Maybe you just make me feel comfortable." Jimmy gazes towards the window as the afternoon sun filters through the curtains. Looking back at Osana, calmly flipping through her phone, Jimmy feels a sort of peace come over him.

"Ya know," Osana says, breaking the silence, "I've never paid much attention to this neighborhood."

Jimmy looks at her with a smirk. "Never paid attention? You've been here your whole life."

"Yeah, I know, but I never really looked at it, just kind of been passing through it. I'm looking at other neighborhoods and they're so nice."

"Oh, really? What are you looking at, some Beverly Hills real estate?"

Osana leans back. "No, but you know, you can see all sorts of places on the phone now. I'm just curious to see other places." She turns to Jimmy. "Do you mind being here, in this area?"

"No, why would I mind? I got you with me."

Osana giggles. "You know what I mean! In Hunts Point. It ain't got the best reputation."

"Yeah, I know what you mean. Think about it. There's some nice coffee shops, pizzerias, and restaurants. There's a library and a bunch of cool stuff around here. It's like a mix of every-thing."

Osana tilts her head. "Maybe. Could be."

"There's even a new dog park. Hey, maybe we'll get a dog, no?"

Osana is startled by his 'we' comment, ignoring it. "I ain't taking care of no dog!"

"Yeah, me neither. Forget the dog. A cat?"

"No, you can't have a cat with a baby in the house!"

"Why not?"

"They take the baby's breath away."

"What are you talking about?"

"I don't know, that's what they say."

"I don't believe that. Sounds like an old wives thing."

Amy starts to cry and Osana knows it is time to put the baby in her crib and leaves to attend to her for a while. Osana comes back to the living room with two quarts of beer, drinking glasses, and a new THC vape and announces. "It's adult time!" as she places all the items on the coffee table in front of the couch.

"Ain't it a little early for beer?"

"Why? You can just vape if you want."

"Maybe a little beer won't hurt." Jimmy cracks the first quart open and fills both glasses. The two of them focus on the vape each taking several tokes off it. The conversation starts in a light tone but becomes bleaker as Jimmy gets more stoned. He jumps to talking about how abysmal his life is. Osana probes him about it. "So, what about your home life?"

Jimmy stops talking and stares at Osana for a minute. "Well, I guess it's time to tell you the truth. I have a wife and two kids."

"Wow, I figured about the wife, but not the kids. How old are they?"

"One's like an infant and my son's five."

"So, you have a baby, too."

"Yeah. She's kind of sick, needs special medicines and stuff."

"Poor baby! I hope she'll be ok."

"Yeah, the doctor told us lots of kids have it and they grow up and all."

"I hope so."

"I get why you've been running back and forth now."

"Yeah, that's it. It's always something. No matter what you do it's never enough. Or I'm wrong all the time."

"Maybe it's just the way—"

"Anyway, I'd rather be here with you. I feel free here."

Osana rests her head on Jimmy's shoulder, and they just stay quiet for a while, until Osana whispers. "Are you comfortable with me?"

Jimmy is feeling inebriated and turns to hug Osana. They begin kissing on the couch, more passionately as time goes on. Until Osana slowly stands up and extends her hand to Jimmy. They giggle a bit as Jimmy stands up and is led down the hallway to the bedroom. Inside, they rush to undress and collapse onto the bed.

The next couple of hours are a blur of tender touches and some very rough acts. Even in his impaired state, Jimmy can tell Osana is much more skilled sexually than he is, and certainly more than his wife. He wonders how many partners Osana has had in her life, but to Jimmy, their lovemaking is not just physical but deeply emotional. This act only solidifies Jimmy's belief that Osana is the one he must be with.

Jimmy lies there looking at Osana so tranquil, her eyes are sparkling with a mix of mischief and affection.

"I can't believe how calm I feel with you," Osana says, laying her head on Jimmy's chest.

"I know," Jimmy agrees, putting his hand under her chin to bring her face to his. "I feel it, too."

They stay wrapped in each other's arms and Jimmy can feel the gentle rise and fall of her breathing. In this quiet moment, he realizes how deeply he cares for Osana. Jimmy lay there gently stroking Osana's hair, a contented smile on his face until falling asleep. As she stirs awake, she looks up with a sleepy, satisfied smile. "Is it morning?" she murmurs, her voice soft and warm.

"No, not yet." Jimmy replies, kissing her forehead. "How are you feeling?"

"Perfect," Osana stretches lazily. "That was amazing, babe."

Jimmy nods, his heart swells with love. "We've got a connection now."

Just then they hear Amy cry from the other room. They look at each other and Osana says. "Ugh, it's feeding time. Back to reality."

Osana gets out of bed, throws some sweatpants and a T-shirt on, and heads out of the room. Jimmy also gets up and starts getting dressed.

When Osana returns Jimmy tells her. "Babe, I hate to do this, but I gotta head out."

Another Woman

Jimmy enters his apartment quietly and tiptoes toward the bedroom. Before he gets there Marie appears out of nowhere startling Jimmy. She has an angry expression on her face. "Jimmy, where have you been?! I've been worried sick!"

"You're the one who said you wanted to be alone. What are you blaming me for?!"

"Oh, it's my fault now. Something's different. What's going on?"

"I went over to a friend's house, we had a few drinks, and I fell asleep for a while. What's the big deal?"

"It is a big deal! And who's this friend? It's a woman, isn't it? I can smell her on you."

"I'm not out with a woman. I'm just hanging out with friends. You act like I'm doing something terrible."

"I can smell her! You're choosing to stay out and party with some whore over being here with your family. What about our marriage?"

"What about it?" Jimmy says as if it is already in the past.

"When you don't come home, I don't know if you're okay, maybe something happened to you. It's like you don't care how I feel."

"I just... I need a break. Things have been stressful, and I have a lot on my mind."

"There's another woman. Just tell me!"

"Stop, you're talking crazy now, It's all in your head, Marie."

"Your family needs to be a priority in your life!"

Jimmy nods and feigns remorse thinking it is the easiest way out of the situation. "Ok, you're right. I've been selfish. I'll work on being more aware of things."

Marie knows he is saying this to appease her but feels like she has no other option than to agree. "Thank you. I just want us to be on the same page. We have bigger problems to deal with, you need to be here. What if there's an emergency with Jeannie and you're not around?"

"You're right... you're right. I'm sorry. I'll be more considerate. Right now, I want to lay down for a while before I get ready for work."

❦ ❦ ❦

Later in the afternoon, Marie, with Jeannie, runs into Gina at the supermarket.

"Hey Marie! How are you? Let me look at that beautiful baby." Gina bends over to tickle Jeannie's chin. "She's really growing, Marie. I think she's gonna be tall."

"Oh, I hope you're right. That'll be nice. So, how you've been?"

Gina motions. "Same stuff, ya know. Work, home, putting up with the hubby, that's about all I do. What about you? You look like something's bothering you; like you didn't sleep last night."

"Well... you're right about that. Jimmy didn't get home until this morning. I was up all night."

"What?! Where was he?" Gina is shocked to hear their marriage may be in trouble.

Marie pauses to think. "How about you come by my place for tea when you're done shopping, and we'll talk?"

"Of course, Marie. I should be done soon."

　　　

Marie sits at her kitchen table with a cup of tea growing cold, stirring it distractedly. Gina is across from her, a concerned look etched on her face.

Gina has always been a pillar of support for Marie. Their friendship has been forged over years of shared laughter and tears and is needed more than ever. Marie takes a deep breath, gathering the courage to voice the turmoil churning inside her. "Gina, I need to ask you something," Marie begins, her voice trembling slightly. "How do you know if your husband is cheating on you?"

Gina's eyebrows knit together in concern. She sets her cup of tea down and leans forward, giving Marie her full attention. "Why are you asking me that?"

Marie's eyes dart away. "Lately, I've noticed some things making me worry. Jimmy's been coming home late; he's distracted all the time, and I can smell a woman on him. I've tried to talk to him about it, but he just brushes it off."

Gina nods, her expression thoughtful. "It sounds like you're going through a lot. I'm glad you're talking about it. There are some signs to look for, but not all of them mean something is wrong.

Marie looks at her friend, desperation in her eyes. "What kinds of signs should I be looking for?"

Gina chooses her words carefully. "First, look out for changes in behavior. If he's suddenly more distant, or avoiding conversations, it could be a red flag. Also, if he's become more secretive about his phone, or if he's guarding his stuff more than usual, that's another thing to watch for."

Marie's mind is straining to understand something she is not equipped to handle. She was only taught the right thing to do in a marriage, never about when it goes wrong. Marie is not even sure she should be talking to Gina about any of this.

Gina continues. "But there might be other explanations for him acting like that. He could be stressed from work, or maybe there's something else going on that's got nothing to do with another woman."

Gina looks at Marie with empathy. "Before jumping to conclusions, try to have an honest conversation with him again. Express how you're feeling without accusing him. Sometimes, people need a nudge to open up about what's really going on in their lives."

Marie agrees, taking in Gina's advice. "I guess I've been so caught up in my fears that I haven't tried to understand his side of things. Maybe I'm being too quick to think the worst."

Gina reaches out and takes Marie's hand. "It's natural to worry, especially when you care about someone. Just remember, communication is key. You owe it to yourself and your relationship to seek the truth gently and openly."

Marie squeezes Gina's hand gratefully. "Thank you, Gina. I'll try to approach it with more understanding. I just hope I'm not being too naïve."

Gina gives her a reassuring smile. "You're not naïve. You're being proactive and caring. That's what matters most. And whatever happens, you've got a friend who's here for you every step of the way."

After Gina leaves Marie spends time in front of the bedroom mirror, brushing her long, chestnut hair. It has been her signature look for years—simple, classic, and comfortable. But she thinks making a change might be something to catch her husband's eye in a new way. She wants to reawaken an ember, to shake up the everyday. Maybe a new hairstyle will be just the thing.

She browses through her magazines. Short, textured cuts, playful waves, and vibrant colors filled the pages. She has always admired bold, confident styles from afar but never dared to try them herself. Now, however, she is ready for a change. She is ready to be brave.

She schedules an appointment with an acquaintance, Linda, a hairstylist with a reputation for bringing out the best in her clients.

⁂

On the day of the appointment, Marie feels a mix of excitement and nerves. She walks into the salon, greeted by the soothing hum of hair dryers and the scent of shampoo. Linda is waiting with a warm smile.

"So, what are we thinking today?" Linda asks, draping a cape over Marie's shoulders.

"I want something... different," Marie says, her eyes scanning the salon's wall of hair inspiration. "I've been thinking about something shorter, maybe with some layers and highlights."

Linda's eyes light up. "I love it! How about we give you a chic bob with some caramel highlights? It'll frame your face beautifully and add a bit of dimension."

Marie's heart jumps at the thought. She okays it, trying to seem more confident than she is. As Linda works, Marie's hair falls away in soft, precise snips. She looks in the mirror, amazed at how different she looks with each passing minute.

The caramel highlights begin to catch the light, giving her a warm glow she has not seen in years.

Marie gasps when Linda spins her around to face the mirror. Her new hairstyle is stunning and full of life. A surge of excitement and pride rushes through her. This is not just about making a change; it is about rediscovering a part of herself she set aside.

※※※

Jimmy arrives home from work, expecting his usual routine of a quiet dinner and regular television shows. As he walks through the door, he freezes for a moment, his eyes widening as he takes in Marie's new look.

"Whoa," he says, his voice filled with genuine surprise. "You look amazing!"

Marie blushes, her heart flutters at the compliment. "Thank you. It was time for a change. Do you like it?" She asks, flipping her hair with her hand.

Jimmy steps closer, "It's not just a change. I don't think I've ever seen you look so good."

Marie glows, with relief and happiness washes over her. "I wasn't sure. I just felt like doing something different. It's been so long, and I thought, why not?"

Jimmy moves closer, gently tucking some hair behind her ear. "It suits you. You look so dazzling. Like you're ready to take on the world."

"Or maybe just cook dinner." she laughs, the sound brightening the room even more. "But seriously, I wanted a change. It feels liberating to just go for it."

Jimmy pretends to study her like a piece of art. "Well, I know you're going to have everyone in the building talking!"

"You really think so?"

"Yes, and let them!" Jimmy shrugs. "You know what they say: life's too short for boring hair."

"Okay, then. You're going to have to take me for dinner again. I want to show off my new look!"

"Absolutely! You can even pick the place this time."

They spend the evening talking, and Jimmy's approval makes Marie feel like she is seeing him with new eyes as well. It is not just about the hairstyle—it is about the self-assurance and joy it brings out in her.

Forget Something?

As days pass Marie is hopeful a page has been turned - until Jimmy stumbles in early one morning. She refuses to admit nothing has changed, convincing herself it is a one-time slip. But as the pattern persists her concern turns from frustration to an all-consuming fear.

Marie stands in the hallway of their apartment waiting to confront him. Even in the dim light, she could see his blood-shot eyes and disheveled clothes. She takes a deep breath, her resolve strengthened. "Morning." her voice steady and sharp.

Jimmy grunts an unintelligible reply, his steps faltering as he heads toward the bedroom. They are now face to face, but Jimmy avoids her stare. The following silence is filled with unspoken words.

"You want to sleep?" Marie breaks the tension.

"Yeah, I do. Can you let me by, please?" Jimmy mumbles, still not looking at her.

"Jimmy," she begins with a firm tone. "We need to talk."

He grimaces, his shoulders tensing. "Can't it wait? I really need to lay down."

"No, it can't wait. How long do you think I'm going to take this?" Marie's voice is rising despite her efforts to stay calm. "You've been coming home drunk more and more often, and I'm worried."

Jimmy's eyes finally meet hers, but they are clouded with a mix of anger and guilt. "I've told you before, Marie, it's just a drink or two with friends. It's nothing to get worked up about."

"A drink or two doesn't explain the way you've been staggering in at all hours, reeking of alcohol, that whore's cheap body spray, and who knows what else you're smoking." Marie shoots back. "It's affecting everything—our home, our life together. I can't keep pretending it's not a problem."

Jimmy's face darkens as he tries to walk past her. "Maybe I just need some space, alright? I didn't come here to be lectured."

"Space?" Marie's voice cracks. "You're avoiding the issue. This isn't just about needing space; it's about you getting out of control."

"I'm not out of control! I'm not happy." Jimmy's voice is rising now.

Marie's eyes flash with hurt. "Oh, so now we're getting to the truth, you're unhappy."

They fall into silence again, this time more profound. Jimmy's posture begins slumping. Marie watches him, her heart aches at the sight of the man she loves looking so defeated.

"I didn't mean to say that." Jimmy admits. "I don't know what I want to say."

"So, you want to separate? Is that it?"

"No... yeah... I don't know. You keep pressuring me for an answer I don't have."

"Well, what am I supposed to do, just stand by and let this shit continue? Watch you fall apart in front of me and the kids? I'm trying, what are you doing?"

Jimmy chuckles. "Yeah right, you thought getting a haircut was going to actually do something."

"That's it, you son of a bitch! You know you have a sick baby here, right?"

"Yeah, I know. You bring it up every chance you get." Jimmy says in a heartless manner.

"Get out! Right now! Get Out! You'd better go get help."

"Whatever. Who gives a fuck." Jimmy snaps as he walks out the door.

⁂

J immy finds himself driving aimlessly with his knuckles white around the steering wheel as he navigates the streets. The first part of the ride is him screaming profanities at no one. As he tires himself out, he begins to think of what his options are. Still furious at Marie he decides whatever comes next, he will not go home. This is partly to teach Marie some kind of lesson, but mostly because of his urge to get high.

He finds himself driving to the grocery store near Osana's hoping he will wind up with her at some point. He parks his car, buys a quart of beer, and drinks it in his car. The beer washes the argument with Marie from his memory. Osana becomes the focus of his mind as the effects of the alcohol begin to fade. He knows he can relax with Osana and indulge in a more potent buzz.

Jimmy enters Osana's building through the broken entrance door and makes his way up to her apartment. After knocking roughly on the door, it opens a few inches. "Did you forget something, babe?" Her face lethargically appears through the opening. "Oh Jimmy? What are you doing here?"

"What'd I forget?" Jimmy slurring his words.

"Nothing, I just thought... Why are you here? Are you drunk?" Osana shifts conversations.

"I just had a couple of beers and was thinking about you, so I figured I'd come by, and we could continue the party, ya know?"

"You definitely look and smell like you started already!" Osana mocks but is alarmed at Jimmy's unpredictable behavior and its risk to her way of life.

"So, can I come in?"

"Um, yeah sure, just give me a minute." Osana closes the door and returns after a couple of minutes. Jimmy leans against the hallway wall to keep his balance.

"Come on in, babe" Osana opens the door and steps out of the way.

"Thanks, babe. I could really use your company. I feel like shit."

"You look like shit!" Osana says laughingly. "You want a beer?"

"Nah, I think I had enough of the liquid stuff. You got the vape or something?"

"Yeah, we can do that." Osana leaves the room for a minute and comes back with a small metal box. Jimmy sits on the couch with Osana next to him.

"Here, you can go first." Osana extends her hand with the vape pen in it.

Jimmy takes it and draws a long toke off it. "Oh, that's just want I needed." Jimmy says as he sinks back into the couch.

They have some small talk for a while until Osana pulls a small plastic bag out of the box and jiggles it in front of Jimmy. "How 'bout some of this? Wanna try?"

"What's that? It looks like heroin or something."

Osana snickers. "No silly, it's just some blow. Go ahead." She prepares four lines of it on a mirror already on the coffee table.

Jimmy hesitates for a moment, realizing this drug is not only highly illegal but will usher in a new level of drug use for him. "Ah, fuck it! Gimme that straw." Jimmy snorts two lines of cocaine. "Wow, that shit straightened me right up! It's like fuckin' magic."

Osana does her two lines and puts the bag back in the box. After some kissing and fondling, they move into the bedroom where they lay in bed. The only light is sunlight coming in from around the closed window blinds.

Osana gets up occasionally to check on Amy. Coming back from one of these breaks she stands next to the bed and looks at Jimmy inquisitively. She takes a sit on the edge of the bed and speaks softly. "You probably think I always drank and did drugs, right?"

"What? No, of course not. What makes you think that?"

"I can tell. People think because I live here, they know about me."

"Osana, I don't know what you're talking about. Did I ever—"

"Do you want to hear it?"

"Hear what? You can tell me anything, you should know that."

Osana steadies herself. "You're only like the second person I ever told this."

Jimmy sits up in bed, his gaze steady and reassuring. "What's going on?"

Osana bites her lip, her hands gripping her knees. "It's how I started with drugs. I'm not proud of it, but I want to tell you."

Jimmy places his hand on Osana's. "Babe, is everything alright?"

"I just want you to know this isn't me. I didn't start this."

"Whatever it is. Just tell me."

"You never met my mother, but she's been an addict since she was young and would turn tricks to keep up with her habit. I guess as she got older some of the tricks wanted a younger girl, so she turned to me."

"Oh my god, babe. I'm so sorry."

"I didn't want to do it. I put up a real fight the first few times. One of the guys told her to get me stoned so I would play along."

Jimmy listens to her speak with a mix of disbelief and sympathy but does not want her to think he is judging her.

"She forced me to get high before the men came over and just left me lying there when they were done. She kept all the money, too. I barely had enough to eat. It only stopped when she went to jail when I was fifteen."

Jimmy is silent for a moment, processing the gravity of what Osana is sharing. "That's horrible. I feel so bad you had to go through that."

"You gonna think different about me now?" Osana probes, her voice barely above a whisper.

"Of course not," Jimmy says firmly. "Thank you for telling me the story. I know it must have been so hard for you."

A sob escapes Osana's lips. Jimmy takes her hands in his, squeezing them gently. "I'm here for you, Osana. You know how I feel about you." The two of them spend a long time silent in each other's arms.

⁂

A few days later Jimmy wants to show Osana how much he cares for her. Knowing that she used to paint back in uncomplicated times he finds an art supply store and goes shopping. He selects a variety of supplies, assorted paint colors, a set of new brushes, and a sketchbook. To top it off, he buys a journal he thinks she could use for jotting down ideas. He carefully packs everything in a box, adding a small note that reads, "For the artist in you."

He shows up at her door with the box. "I've got a surprise for you!" he says, his eyes full of excitement.

Osana has him come in and they go into the living room where Jimmy places the box on the coffee table. "Go ahead. Open it."

She sits down and opens the box; her eyes narrow. "Paint supplies? What am I gonna do with this?"

"What do you mean? Get back to painting, of course."

"Paint what? The apartment? What are you talking about?"

"Paint like you used to do." Jimmy barks as he points to her art on the walls. "Didn't you say—"

"I ain't got time for that."

"You should make time. It would be good for you." Jimmy stands there confused trying to understand her reaction.

Osana turns and starts going through her phone. Jimmy does not realize his gesture has unintentionally stirred memories of the difficult times in her life.

"You know what? Forget it. I'm sorry I went through all the trouble of buying this shit." Jimmy grabs the box and throws it in the closet near the entrance door.

"What the fuck do I bother for?" Jimmy shouts as he storms out of the apartment to go sit in his car. "Fuck her. I gotta calm down."

Drag It Out?

Marie sits at the kitchen table. She dropped Bobby off at school and Jeannie is sleeping comfortably in her crib. She is deep in thought, gazing at a family portrait in the hallway. Jimmy left a voicemail at 4:00 a.m. saying he needs to talk. She almost did not recognize his voice, it sounded emotionless, and she knew this conversation was not going to be a congenial one. Suddenly the phone rings, slicing through the silence. Marie's heart skips a beat. She glances at the caller ID — Jimmy.

"Hello."

"Hello, Marie." His voice has a bleakness she has not heard before. "I, I need to talk to you about something."

Marie's heart sinks. "I know. It sounds important."

Jimmy clears his throat. "I've been thinking a lot lately. About you and me."

Marie's fingers tighten around the phone. "What about?"

There is a pause, Marie thinks of saying something to fill the void, but keeps quiet, not wanting to say the wrong thing. His words come out slowly, methodically, as if he has rehearsed them. "I haven't been happy for a while. I've tried to figure out what's wrong, but I can't."

She feels a lump form in her throat. "Jimmy, if there's something wrong, we can work through it."

"It's more than that, Marie. This isn't about fixing things. I don't know, maybe we're just not meant to be together anymore."

She struggles to catch her breath. "Are you saying you want a divorce?"

There is a long silence at the other end. "Not really, not yet." Jimmy finally says. "I've been seeing someone else. I didn't plan for this to happen, but it did. It made me realize I need to be honest with myself and with you. Maybe I just need a break."

Marie's vision blurred with tears. "So, what happens now?"

"I want to be fair," Jimmy says coldly. "I'm going to move out. I'll help with the finances, and I'll make sure you and the kids are taken care of. But I think it's best like this."

Marie closes her eyes, trying to stave off the storm of emotions crashing over her. "What about Jeannie's medical things?"

"I'm going to make sure that's covered." Jimmy tells her with no intention of following through on this promise.

"Are you quitting your job, too?"

"No, no I wouldn't do that."

Hearing that did little to ease her pain. "When are you coming back home to discuss this in person?"

"I think it's better if we do this over the phone for now. I don't want to drag this out."

Marie senses anger growing inside her. "Drag it out? I'm your wife and your kids are here."

"Yeah, I know, but—"

"Are you coming to get your things?"

"Well... leave me a message when you're not going to be there for like an hour, and I'll come by."

With those final words, Jimmy hangs up. Marie stares at the phone, her mind reeling. The life she envisioned for herself, and her children, is abruptly shattered. She takes a shaky breath looking around the home they have built together—at the memories mounted on the walls, the laughter, the tears. The realization of what she needs to do next settles over her like a heavy cloak. For now, she needs to stay strong—for her children. The road ahead is going to be challenging, but she is determined to face it head-on, one step at a time.

Jimmy tells Osana about the phone call later. She recognizes he is under her influence but is not completely sure this is what she wants. She does have some kind feelings for him, but Carlo is always in the back of her mind. She chooses to test Jimmy. "Jimmy, you always bring me some nice things when you come by."

"Hey, I try to not show up empty-handed."

"Yeah, but you never bring anything for Amy, how come?"

"I brought her stuff before. Does she need something now?"

"She always needs something all the time Jimmy, she's just a baby. I mean, you know I'm not just about material shit, but she needs things, too."

"Yeah, of course. Remember I have a baby."

"You take care of her, so if you want to be part of us here you gotta do something for Amy. Don't that make sense?"

"I get it, you're right."

"It's not all about getting high and fuckin', ya know." Osana says sarcastically.

Jimmy jokes. "Oh, I was hoping it was!"

Osana pinches his nose playfully. "No kidding!"

"Haha! But seriously I'll start doing that, I'm sorry."

Jimmy moves to the living room and stands looking out the front window for quite a long time. He needs to be alone with his thoughts and speculate if he is taking the right path. His mind is tangled in a web of uncertainty, only wanting to find a way out of the darkness he feels.

As he glances through the glass down at the street, he can see couples laughing, their faces lit with genuine joy. Jimmy envies them, wishing he could feel affection like that with someone. Looking back on his life he understands he has never experienced anything close to it. Maybe life is supposed to be repetitive, he wonders. It would be the safe path to take, even if it left him unfulfilled. And there are the children to think of. He does not want to feel guilty about abandoning them.

ⴲⴲⴲ

Marie sits at home in silence, her mind is flustered since Jimmy's call. She decides she needs to talk to someone and calls Gina. The phone rings a few times before Gina's voice comes through, warm and familiar. "Hey, Marie! How's it going?"

Marie's throat tightens. "Nothing worked." she manages to get out.

"What didn't work?" Gina's voice shifts instantly to concern. "Are you okay?"

Marie inhales deeply, but all she could feel is the emptiness of a love that has vanished. "No, I'm not okay. Jimmy left me."

A long gap follows. Gina can hear Marie's breath through the phone, waiting, uncertain, before she speaks. "Marie, what do you mean? What happened?"

Marie tries hard to hold back the tears. "He called me and said he's seeing someone else now and he's not coming home. Just like that. I knew there was trouble, but never thought he'd do this to me, to us."

Gina's voice filled with sadness. "Oh, I'm so sorry. I don't even know what to say. I can't imagine what you must be feeling right now."

"I don't know either. I just... I can't stop thinking about everything. All those years together. And now? It's like it was all for nothing." Marie cannot hold the tears back any longer as the pain washes over her. "What did I do so wrong, Gina? I tried, I really tried. I thought we were going to work it out."

Gina stays silent for a moment, giving Marie time to cry, before responding gently, "You didn't do anything wrong. Sometimes people just change. I know it's not easy to hear, but it's not because of you. You're not the one who chose this."

Marie wipes her face, sniffling. "I just don't know how to handle this. I feel like I've lost everything."

"You're strong, and you're loved. You have me. You have so many people who care about you. I'll be here. You don't have to go through this alone." Gina tries to motivate her.

The words are a small comfort, but they help. Gina has always been there for her, even in the dark moments.

"I just want to crawl under a rock and die" Marie admits, her voice barely above a whisper.

"Don't talk like that. You still have the kids to think of." Gina replies. "But you don't have to do it alone. I'll come over. We can sit together, have some tea, talk, or just be quiet. Whatever you need."

Marie sniffles again, feeling a sense of relief. "You'll come over?"

"Of course. I'm on my way now, okay? Don't worry about a thing. I'm not going anywhere."

Those words touch Marie's heart but do little to make the pain go away. "Thank you. I don't know what I'd do without you."

"You'll never have to find out. I'm always here for you."

As the call ends, Marie sits in the quiet of her home, the weight of her heartbreak still heavy.

* * *

Jimmy's phone rings as he drives back to Osana's from the liquor store. He looks at it and sees 'Mom' on the screen. He immediately feels a knot form in his stomach. "Fucking phones! Whoever invented this fucking thing?!"

He groans but swipes to answer. "Hi, Ma."

"Jimmy," she says, in a displeased tone. "It's your mother. I guess I have to be the one to call you every time."

"Sorry, I've just been really busy."

"You're always busy when I call. When was the last time I heard from you? You never check in. You can't take five minutes to call your mother?"

Jake rubbed his temples, trying to keep his patience. "I'm sorry, ma. I really am. I've just got a lot on my plate."

"Why" What's going on with you?"

"Ya know, just work, home, back to work."

"Well, you're just a garbage man. How busy can you be?"

"Gee, thanks. I really appreciate that comment. And you wonder why I don't call."

"Anyway, how's Marie and my grandkids I never see?"

Jimmy's frustration grows. He knows telling her the truth would give her more to criticize him for. "They're all great. Everyone is doing fine."

"I'm getting older every day, and I don't even know what's going on in your life. I get more updates from my friend down the block than I do from my own son."

Jimmy tries to respond but gets cut off.

"Do you even care about me and your father anymore? It's like you're just out there living your life, ignoring your family like we don't matter."

"Ma, I'm not ignoring you guys," Jimmy says softening his voice. "I just trying to make a living and take care of things."

"It sounds like you're just sitting there, letting life pass by. You never even try to make something of yourself. What happened to the son I used to know?"

"When did you ever know me?" Jimmy thinks to himself but dares not express it. "I'm trying," he says apologizing. "I'm really trying. It just feels like nothing is going right."

"Maybe you should try harder," she shoots back. "You're like your father, always having an excuse."

"I'm sorry," he grumbles, feeling like he is sinking. "I'll call more. I promise."

"That would be nice. Can you come by one day with Marie and the kids, so I can see them?"

"Yeah, sure. I'll talk to her, and we'll pick a day. I'll call you to let you know."

"Let's see how long I have to wait for that."

"Listen ma, I gotta run. I'm in the middle of something." Jimmy is nearing his breaking point with this call and needs to get off quickly.

"Well, I'll let you go. Bye."

"Bye ma, we'll talk soon."

Jimmy sits there for a long time staring at the phone in his hand. Her words always make him feel small, and insignificant, like he somehow failed everyone.

J

immy and Osana sit in her living room on a late afternoon, neither one of them talking much, until Osana turns to say. "It's Friday night. We doing anything?"

"I told you. I don't have much money right now. I'm waiting for another paycheck to come through."

"I ain't just gonna sit here tonight doing nothing." she says with an attitude.

"I can go get us some beers and Chinese food and just chill for the night. How's that?"

"I think we need a little bit more than some beers. Can't ya go see Spark?"

"I don't have money for that, I said."

Osana pauses and thinks for a minute. "Well... I can get us some money."

"How ya gonna do that?"

"There's an older guy I know who likes to spend time with me. If I hang out with him a couple of hours, he'll throw me like $100 or whatever."

"Oh, c'mon! I ain't going for that. With you?"

"He don't do sex or anything; he just wants to talk for a while, sometimes I have to rub his neck a little, that's it."

"I don't know. It doesn't sound like a good idea to me." Jimmy does not like the idea of having another man spend time with Osana. He is also naïve about what this situation may involve, making him very uneasy.

"You got a better idea? Nothing's gonna happen, I'm telling you."

"Where am I going" And what about Amy?"

"You guys just hang in her room for a while."

"I don't know, this sounds fucked up to me."

"Believe me, it's ok. He's an old man. You'll see."

"All you think about is money, huh?'

"Yeah, what do you think you're here for." Osana slips by saying this but tries to make a joke of it. "Ha! Look at your face. I'm just playing with you."

"Yeah, right you are. Fuck it, what the hell. Call him."

Osana goes into the kitchen with her cell phone and makes the call. Jimmy is trying to listen in, but she's talking too low. Osana comes back into the living room and tells Jimmy. "Ok, he'll be here in two hours."

"Fine, whatever."

"You gonna get Chinese food?"

Jimmy agrees and makes a run to the takeout place on the next block. When he returns the two of them sit in the living to watch a movie with dinner. As they are finishing up, the intercom rings.

The Old Guy

"**O**h shit, Jimmy, he's here." Osana springs up and tells Jimmy to take Amy into her room and he can watch something on the tablet.

Jimmy stands and says to Amy. "C'mon, let's go to your room." as he picks her up out of the stroller. "I'll show you some funny YouTube videos you might get a kick out of. Mommy has to talk to a friend for a while."

Osana laughs as she folds up the stroller and puts it in the closet. "You're ridiculous! Like she knows what you're saying."

Jimmy stops quickly in the kitchen and takes two bottles of beer out of the refrigerator. He and Amy go into her room, and he hears a knock on the apartment door. He tries to keep as quiet as possible so he can hear what is going on in the living room. Osana says she is well acquainted with this person, but Jimmy does not trust him.

Amy finally falls asleep allowing Jimmy to stand up and press his ear against the bedroom wall. He can hear Osana and the man talking about how the neighborhood has changed, old friends, and some other drivel; nothing to get upset over.

Suddenly their voices get much lower and Jimmy has a hard time hearing what is going on. He presses his ear against other walls with no luck, so presses his ear to the door. "Are those sucking sounds I'm hearing?" He mumbles to himself. "What the fuck is she doing?!"

Pressing even harder against the door. He doesn't hear talking anymore but can hear the man moaning as the sucking noises get louder. Jimmy is certain about what she is doing and is infuriated. He is screaming in his head. 'That mother fucker! She's giving him a blowjob right there in the living room with me and her daughter here!'

Questions spin around his brain. "Do I go out there and throw the scumbag out? Keep my mouth shut and just stay here? What the fuck do I do?" Being in this situation is beyond his experience.

Surprisingly he begins thinking about the money and drugs and cannot believe himself. "Holy shit, what the fuck is wrong with me? What am I becoming?" The jolt of his compliance in this situation seems to invalidate his anger and decides to go sit on the bed until the man leaves.

He sits numb and questioning his part in all this. He feels like his mind is separated from his body, floating in space somewhere foreign. After what seems like hours a knocking on the bedroom door jolts him out of it. "Yeah, coming." He says as he gets up and opens the door and sees Osana.

The two of them stand there looking at each other. Jimmy is still trying to figure out if he's going to say something about the oral sex. Until he notices she is under the influence of something. "You guys got high?"

"He had a little blow on him."

"Nothing for me?" Jimmy says somewhere between disappointment and anger.

"No, I couldn't. He was holding onto it like it was gold."

"So, I went through all this shit for nothing?"

"What shit? What are you talking about?" Osana holds up folded twenty-dollar bills.

"What are you pissed off about? I told you." she says angrily.

"I'm sorry, but you didn't tell me everything, ya know."

"It's like whatever, Jimmy." As she pushes the money into her pocket. "You want the rest of this beef with broccoli?"

Jimmy stands there in disbelief and concedes. "Yeah, I could eat." Jimmy sits down at the kitchen table and eats out of the takeout container.

"I'm gonna take a quick shower."

"Yeah, ok." Jimmy sits there eating still dazed about what has transpired. "I'm gonna go lay down for a while when you're done."

When Osana comes out of the bathroom a short while later, no words are spoken. Jimmy heads to the bedroom.

Osana positions herself curled up on the couch in her sweats with a bottle of beer in one hand and her phone in the other. She is speaking with Bella for a while when the conversation turns to Jimmy, and Osana's attitude becomes critical. Bella questions what is going on between them.

Osana sighing. "You won't believe this guy sometimes."

"Oh no, what happened?"

Osana leans back, closing her eyes as she gathers her thoughts. Her voice takes on a harsh edge. "He's so inconsiderate and like disrespectful. I mean, I don't like the way he thinks about me lately."

"What do you mean? Like what?"

"He thinks my place is a fuckin' crack den, he can just get high here and fuck me whenever he can get his dick up! And now he wants to fuck up what I got going on."

"You gotta straighten that shit out with him."

"Yeah, when I gotta do my stuff, he gets pissed off or whatever."

"Ugh, that's so fucked up."

"I mean it's nice he cares and all, I kinda like it, but don't be too much."

"Does he know he's fucking your plans up?"

"He always says he's sorry, but it's like I gotta tell him when to say it. I feel like I'm just a slut and drug dealer to him and I'm not getting everything I want."

"So, what are you going to do about it?"

"I don't know. I gotta talk to him. I mean, he does give me some pretty good cash, but it just makes me mad sometimes." Osana takes a big gulp from her beer.

Bella remains silent on the other end for a while as she tries to process the situation. After all, tapping men for money and drugs is their way of life, but Osana is taking things personally. Allowing a man too far into her life is outside of Bella's thought process, throwing out an impractical platitude. "Well, what are you going to do, it happens."

Osana appreciates this situation is not something Bella can truly comprehend and tries to make her understand her position better. "Yeah Bella, I know that. This government money ain't nearly enough, so it's the game we gotta play, but we still gotta be treated right." Osana pauses. "Maybe part of it is my fault. I let him get too comfortable. I let him in too much."

"Sounds like he ain't just some guy to you. Do you like him?"

"I did for a while, but that shit is wearing off pretty quick." Osana likes being in a relationship, but Jimmy is too much of a hassle for her.

"Kick him to the curb! What are you waiting for? I'll come over there and do it. I don't give a fuck!"

"No Bella, we all know you don't give a fuck, but I'll take care of it."

Ok, talk to him and see where he stands, that's all."

"Yeah, I guess that's what I should do, first anyways."

"Whatever you decide, just make sure it's what's best for you. And remember, I'm here for you no matter what."

"Thanks, Bella. I will." Osana smiles, feeling a minor sense of comfort from her friend's support. The conversation drifts to lighter topics as time goes on.

In the quiet moments after the call, Osana sits alone thinking about what she should do. The relationship is more complicated than Osana led Bella to believe, she does have some feelings for Jimmy. She decides to talk to him and see where things go for a while more.

The Jimmy Conversation

Danny pulls his personal vehicle into the sanitation yard to prepare for another day of work. As he walks from the parking lot to the office area he runs into Mark.

"Good morning, Danny. How ya doing?"

"Hey, Mark, ya know, same shit. How 'bout you?"

"I'm ok. Actually, I was thinking of Jimmy this morning. You wanna get coffee after work to see if there's anything we can do?"

Danny half-jokingly answers. "Just coffee?" They chuckle.

"Yep, sorry Danny, just coffee."

"I'm just playing. Yeah, of course. I'm sure he can use a friend or two right about now."

"Great. I'll meet you at the diner."

Mark and Danny go through their routines for the day trying to grasp what Jimmy could be going through. If they could understand that they might know how to help him.

***

Mark gets to the diner first and orders a coffee and a slice of pie. Danny joins him about ten minutes later. The waitress comes over to get his order. "What will you have?" She asks.

"Just a coffee." Danny tells her.

"That's all?"

"Well, you could put a shot of something stronger in there, if you got."

"I'm sorry—"

Mark interrupts. "He's just joking with you. Never mind him."

They go over some other work issues, as the waitress brings Danny his coffee.

Mark starts the conversation. "So, you spend more time with him than probably anybody, what do you think is going on?"

Danny takes a sip of his coffee and puts the mug down with a sigh. "I don't know what to do about him. He's a tough guy to get a good take on. He doesn't say much about his personal life, but he was acting strange before all this shit started."

"Yeah. I mean, I know for a while he was showing up late, but it turned into not showing up at all."

"I thought it was just a rough patch with the old lady." Danny pauses. "To tell the truth, shit like this happened twice before."

"How do you know that?"

"Because I'm the one who had to get him back under control. He got obsessed with a couple of women before, but nothing like this."

Mark shakes his head, clearly bothered. "Why? What happened?"

"The same kind of shit. Last time he got hung up on some young chick in the coffee shop we used to go to and I had to have a couple talks with him."

"And he stopped?"

Danny lets out a short snicker. "Only after her boyfriend and a couple other guys rough him up a bit."

"Oh shit. I had no idea he was like that."

"It's not just that. I've been hearing things. People on the route are telling me shit. I figured he was just banging some broad, but she's got him involved with drugs, too."

"Drugs? That's serious shit. I didn't realize it was that bad."

"Yeah, me neither. I thought maybe he was just depressed again or something. But the more I know there's something deeper going on."

"Have you tried talking to him directly? Maybe he's just waiting for someone to reach out."

"I've tried, Mark. I approached him the last time I saw him, just to see if he was okay. He brushed me off, said he was fine. But I know he's not. He was rundown and irritable. I feel so bad for the guy."

"It's tough. He doesn't seem to be even trying to keep it together, and it's clearly taking a toll. If he's using, it's probably hard for him to admit it."

Danny shows his frustration. "I want to help, but I don't know how. I'm not a 'warm and fuzzy' kind of guy or anything. I don't want to make things worse by pushing him too hard."

"Maybe next time either of us sees him we can suggest he see someone, a professional. The department has an Employee Assistance Program. We could point him in that direction."

"That's a good idea. The problem is when are we going to see him next."

"Good point, Danny. We're gonna have to keep an eye out and be prepared to step in right away.

"I just hope he can get the help he needs before it's too late."

"Yeah, he's just lucky we work for a big, bloated bureaucracy and we can cover for him." Danny teases.

"True, but that ain't going to last much longer." Mark pauses. "You don't drink in front of him, do you?"

"What? On the job? No friggin' way. You trying to get me in trouble?" Danny says jokily.

"Ha, funny." Mark says lightly. "What about his wife and kids? What are they going through?"

"I thought about them, too but I don't know Marie, so I feel uncomfortable stopping by their place. We know the little girl is sick, not much else."

"Should we reach out to her? Or maybe it's too soon." Mark questions.

"I'm not sure. She could get embarrassed knowing that we know what's going on. Let's wait a while and see what happens."

"Ok, if we don't get any good news soon, I'll go see her." Danny proposes.

Mark adds. "I'm going to call him to warn him that HR is going to pick up on his attendance sooner or later. Maybe that might shake him up a bit."

They finish their coffees in silence.

Insufficient Funds

Jimmy is heading back to Osana's and gives her a call on the way. "Hey, babe I'm headed to you now and thought you might need me to bring something?"

"I can't think of anything, but you can't come for a while. Got some things going on. We'll talk in a few hours. I'll call you." Osana quickly disconnects the call.

Jimmy is irritated and wonders what this is about. Osana is always been a bit mysterious, but this is unusual. The vague message and her hurried tone make Jimmy's curiosity gnaw at him. He tries to call her again, but it goes straight to voicemail.

He decides to head to Osana's apartment hoping to surprise her and find out what is going on. It is getting dark when he arrives at her building. Jimmy is surprised to find out the front door is working so he buzzes, but there is no response.

Frustrated but determined, Jimmy waits for someone to leave, he slips in, and goes up to Osana's door. His knocks grow louder with each attempt, but still no answer. He thinks she might have another man inside or doing something else she does not want him to know about. It cannot be good.

As he is about to turn away, he hears muffled voices from inside. He pauses, unsure of what to do. Just as he is about to knock again the door opens a crack. Osana's face appears, her eyes wide with a mix of surprise and worry.

"Jimmy, what are you doing here?" her voice low and hurried.

"I came to see you. You didn't answer my calls. What's going on?" Jimmy's tone is a mix of concern and frustration.

Osana hesitates, then groans. "Jimmy seriously, you have to get out of here."

Jimmy peers around her to see inside and there are several men scattered around, their faces tense. They are working on something he cannot see. Something more than a casual gathering is taking place.

Osana steps into the hallway so they can talk privately. "Jimmy, you know the guys you deal with on the street?"

"Yeah, I don't see them—"

"These are the guys they get their shit from. They come here to cook, and package shit up sometimes."

"What do you get out of this?"

Osana just answers. "They take care of me."

Jimmy's eyes widen. "They give you some of the shit?"

Osana takes a deep breath. "I'll tell you more later, but you need to get out of here. These guys aren't fuckin' around. They don't want to be seen."

Jimmy's heart pounds. "And what if the police come? What if something goes wrong?"

"That's why I have to keep you away. Just come back later...please."

Jimmy feels helpless, also somewhat relieved it is not another man. "Ok, give me a call later, but you have to let me in on what's going on."

"I will, I will. Just please go."

Jimmy begrudgingly turns and exits the building.

He first stops at the corner grocery store and buys himself a pint of beer to keep occupied as he walks the streets without direction. Still wounded over what just occurred, he mumbles various insults and grievances as he puts one foot in front of the other.

"Mother fuckers, I bet they're all laughing and getting stoned up there and I'm on the street like some jerk off. They'll all get theirs one day, one day real soon. Fuck 'em all."

"**O**h wait!" Jimmy says out loud. He remembers a paycheck should have been direct deposited into his account and begins looking for a bank with an ATM machine.

"I'll show those fuckers what a party is! Get me some cash, some blow, and maybe I can find a couple of hoes to enjoy it with, too."

A bank comes into view and Jimmy quickens his steps. He thinks about the happenings that will follow withdrawing cash. Jimmy is so excited he fails to take one detail into account. When he and Marie got married, they were guided by some fundamental principles. One of them being a couple must have all their funds in one account or they are not truly married. This means Jimmy has no accounts solely in his name.

Up to this point, Jimmy steered away from withdrawing too much cash at one time because Marie would gripe about it. The days of those concerns are behind him now. He has lost all concern for what Marie thinks or how it affects his family.

At last, he stands in front of the ATM. The soft hum of the streets played a low, rhythmic background to his thoughts. Impatiently Jimmy slips his card into the machine. The screen comes to life and the machine begins its familiar animations, Jimmy punches in his PIN and selects the amount he wants. But instead of the usual 'Processing' message, the machine displays a blunt 'Insufficient Funds.' Jimmy studies the screen convinced he is misreading it. He re-enters his PIN and selects the amount again, his actions frantic now, but the message remains unchanged.

He marches away to find the next ATM and discovers one a few blocks away. It produces the same disheartening result; his frustration surges.

He needs to speak with someone who could provide answers. He turns on his heel and heads back to the first bank, which is about to close. Jimmy approaches the counter, his face full of concern. The teller, a young woman with an empathetic smile, listens as he explains the problem.

"I'm sorry to hear that, sir." she says after checking his account. Her fingers tapped the keyboard with a precise rhythm. "It appears the other account holder has withdrawn the funds."

Jimmy's anxiety changes to anger upon hearing the news. "How can the bank allow that?!"

"Sir, it's a joint account, either individual is allowed to deposit or withdraw funds." The teller's tone is firm.

"Can't you put it back or something?"

"Sir, There's no way—"

"Ah, fuck you, too!" Jimmy grabs his ATM card, storms out of the bank, and calls Marie.

"Yes, Jimmy." Marie answers, aware of why he is calling.

"What the hell did you do with our account?" Jimmy screams into the phone.

Marie keeps herself relatively calm. "What did I do? You're the one who's been draining it."

"I took some money out, so what?"

"So, I still need to run a family here, remember?"

"That's my money! You never put shit in there!"

"Oh, here we go. I need money for serious things, like our sick daughter. While you're running around with some whore. Your daughter's been getting worse and how am I supposed to pay for her medical stuff?"

Jimmy's anger deflates. "She's getting worse?"

"Yes, she's sick all the time now," Marie starts to cry. "And I'm the only one caring for her. You don't even give a shit."

This strikes Jimmy hard, but the craving to get high overshadows everything else. "Ok, do what you gotta do." Jimmy says in a low voice and hangs up on the call. Jimmy spends the next several minutes pacing back and forth with only one thought in his head – how is he going to get high.

The guilt Marie left him with soon turns to resentment. "That fucking bitch! She thinks she's gonna fuck me up tonight? Fuck her! I know where I can get some shit." Jimmy thinks if he can find Spark and get some credit he can party himself. So, he sets out on a new journey.

Jimmy falters through the night, his hands trembling and his heart pounding with an almost unbearable urgency. The addiction gnaws at him like a rabid beast.

As Jimmy walks by the window of a vacant store he catches a glimpse of his reflection. A once clean-cut appearance is disheveled and worn. His face is thin, his clothes hang looser on his frame. For a fleeting moment, he wonders how he became so hollow and desperate. None of it matters to him right now, though.

He has already hit the usual spots, the places where Spark would often be. But tonight, he is nowhere to be found. Jimmy's phone is dead, cutting off his lines of communication.

Jimmy's steps grow more erratic. He turns a corner and sees a group of homeless people huddled around a small folding table smoking cigarettes and sharing a few cans of beer. He approaches them. "Have you guys seen Spark? I need to find him. Please."

The mix of ragged men with indifferent faces exchange glances. One of them, a younger man with a cigarette dangling from his lips, shrugs. "Sorry, man. Haven't seen anybody around."

Jimmy mutters a thank you, though he barely hears it himself, and continues on. He walks over to the park where he used to meet Spark at times, but it is empty. Jimmy leans against a graffiti-covered wall, trying to collect his thoughts.

An unexpected movement catches his eye. A figure steps out of a shadowy doorway—a wiry man with eyes that dart around with practiced paranoia. Jimmy approaches the man. "You know where I can find Spark?"

The man smiles, but something is unsettling about it. Jimmy's nerves are already on edge. "Spark? Yeah, I know him. But he's not in the mood for visitors right now."

Jimmy's hope wavers, but desperation pushes him forward. "Please, I need to see him. I've been looking for him."

The man's expression softens, but only slightly. He takes a long drag from his cigarette before speaking. "I know where you can get some shit."

"I'm not buying right now."

"Oh, no money, huh? I'll give you five bucks for a blowjob. How's that?"

Jimmy stands there staring at this person not knowing how to react, until the man speaks again.

"Nah, I'm just fuckin' with you, man. You can't take a joke?"

"Not really in the mood. Do you know—"

"I know a lot of shit, man. I've seen you around. You tight with Spark?"

"Yeah, yeah, we're tight. I know the guy."

"I guess you're cool." The man tells Jimmy an address, his tone a mix of pity and disdain. "Be quick. Spark don't sit still for long."

Jimmy thanks the man and hurries away, his mind a whirl of anticipation. The address leads him to a rundown building four blocks away, it seems like miles to Jimmy. He approaches the building hesitantly, each step echoing in the silence of the night. Most of the streetlights are not working and the ones that are cast long shadows stretching out to grab him as he moves forward. He reaches the entrance, a metal door that looks as though it has not been painted in decades. He knocks, the sound almost lost in the darkness. The door creaks open a sliver, revealing a pair of bloodshot eyes peeking out. "Who you?" comes a gruff voice from inside.

"It's Jimmy. I'm looking for Spark."

"Who the fuck are you?"

"You know me, man. I've seen you with him before."

"Wait a fucking minute."

Jimmy assumes he has gone to check with Spark, and after a couple of minutes, the door swings wide open. Jimmy steps inside, the dim light from a single hanging bulb illuminating a dingy hallway. The air is thick with the scent of mold, and stale smoke.

He is led down the corridor to a small, cluttered room. Spark sits at a rickety table, surrounded by half-empty bottles and crumpled papers. His eyes, sharp and calculating, meet Jimmy's with a mixture of recognition and disbelief. "What the fuck are you doing here?" Spark's voice suggests he is not in the mood for pleasantries.

"I've been looking for you," Jimmy says, his voice cracking slightly. "I need—"

"Need? What do you need?" Spark cuts him off, leaning back in his chair. "We ain't friends, ya know. No freebies. You gotta pay."

Jimmy looks down at the floor. "That's what I wanted to talk to you about. I'm kind of short today. Maybe I can get something on credit. I just need—"

Spark's patience snaps. "You think I'm running a fuckin' charity here?! You come to me empty-handed wanting a favor? You're risking a lot just by being here."

Jimmy's heart sinks. He sees the finality in Spark's eyes, the message is clear he is not getting any leniency tonight. "Please," his voice breaking. "I'm begging you. Just whatever you got."

Spark's gaze turns to one of the other men in the room. "You believe this piece of shit? What fuckin' balls!" Looking back at Jimmy. "You know I could kill you right here, right now, don't you?"

"Yeah, I know. I didn't mean anything."

Spark laughs ever so slightly, but only for a moment. He picks up a small bag from under the table and tosses it towards Jimmy. "Take it and get the fuck out. But this is the last time. Next time, you come prepared or don't come at all."

Jimmy grabs the bag clutching it to his chest. "Thank you. I swear, I'll pay you back. I just—"

"Enough talk," Spark interrupts, waving him off. "Just go."

Jimmy rushes out of the room. Just as he is exiting one of the men punches Jimmy in the back of the head. Jimmy falls forward putting his hands out just in time to prevent his face from hitting the floor. As regains his footing again he hears the men behind him laughing. He dares not turn around heading out faster than before, barely registering the grime of the walls or the pests running past his feet. All that matters is the bag he holds and the promise of relief it contains. He gets back into the night and rushes back to his car. He partakes in Spark's charity and finishes his last can of beer until exhaustion sets in and he falls asleep.

Deep Paranoia

I t's morning, he drives over to the gas station, charges his phone, and cleans up in the bathroom. Feeling a little better he buys himself a coffee and buttered roll and sits in the car eating, sickened by the previous night's events. He never imagined he could sink to such depths, a beggar, and not even for food, but pitiful drugs.

He is just about to call Osana to see if he is allowed there when his phone begins ringing. He does not recognize the number. "Ah! who the fuck is this now?" he answers hesitantly "Hello."

"Hey Jimmy, It's Mark."

Jimmy sits up straight and does his best to speak in an ordinary manner. "Oh hey, Mark. I didn't recognize the number. What's up?"

"I'm calling from my cellphone; I didn't want to use the office line. To get right to it, I'm kind of concerned. You've been missing days lately and I was wondering if there's an issue."

Jimmy is taken aback Mark is calling him about this and needs to come up with a story fast.

"Oh yeah, I meant to call you. Ya know, I got the sick kid and everything. We gotta bring her to doctors and tests and all that stuff."

"Yeah, I was figuring that might be part of it, but Danny also mentioned there may be some other stuff going on."

"Danny? What does he think he knows?"

"Well, he didn't give me any details, but I was thinking there was some other personal shit happening. You guys work in the truck together so I thought he might know what's going on."

"No, no everything else is fine, just the shit with my kid." Jimmy must hide the truth and continues to give excuses.

"Ok, if that's what you say, but the reason I'm calling is HR's gonna pick up on your days out soon, so I'm just trying to help you out, that's all.

"I appreciate it, Mark. Thanks. I guess I'll have to explain it to them when I get the call."

"Yeah, I guess so. Hey, we all got bills and credit cards, right?" Mark says to ease the tension.

"Ok, well thanks again Mark, but I'm good, really."

"Alright, but if you need anything, please save this number and call me."

"Sure, will do."

After the call ends, Jimmy sits there, motionless, trying to process the news. It is not just about the job or the money; the uncertainty is overwhelming. He is on the verge of tears when something Mark said comes back to him. "Fuck! I'm an idiot. Credit cards! How could I not think of that." Jimmy remembers he has two credit cards in his wallet, and can use them to get cash. He heads straight back to the bank's ATM and extracts the maximum from one of them, holding the other for the next predicament. This lifts his spirits greatly; it is time to call Osana. "Hey, babe, everything all clear there?"

"Sure, you wanna come over?"

"You bet. I'll be there in a little while."

"Is everything okay?"

"Everything's rainbows and unicorns now! See you in a bit."

Jimmy stops by the gas station again to get gas and clean himself up a little more. The next stops are the grocery store to buy beer and some items for breakfast. Then it is back to Spark's where Jimmy knocks confidently this time.

※ ※ ※

T he door opens wide this time. "What the fuck you want now? A punch in the face this time?" says Spark's underling.

"No, I'm here to buy!" Jimmy announces. "Let me in."

"You think 'cause you got money, you got balls now?"

Jimmy scales back his attitude. "I just want to see Spark, that's all."

The young man turns and starts walking down the hallway, Jimmy follows until they reach the back room.

Spark looks up from what he is doing and shakes his head. "You don't quit, do you?"

"I got money to pay you for the other shit and get some more."

"You know I'm hanging here to keep it cool. I ain't supposed to be selling, right?"

"Yeah, I get that, but you know me, c'mon."

Spark looks at the young man standing next to Jimmy. "I can't believe this fucking guy." then turns back to Jimmy. "How much you got?"

Jimmy places several bills on the table, Spark picks it up and counts it.

"Ok, ok we can work with this. Gonna be a good time, huh?"

"Yeah, I hope so. Should be a good one."

Spark doles out a mix of drugs to Jimmy, who picks them up quickly and puts them in his pocket. "Thanks, I appreciate it."

"I don't give a shit what you appreciate. I see you back here again I'm gonna put a bullet in your face."

Jimmy is ready and gets himself to Osana's, where she greets him tenderly. "I'm sorry about last night, babe. It's just those guys don't like—"

"It's fine. Don't worry about it." Jimmy says as he hands her the beer and food.

"Ok, so what do you want to do? Did you eat?"

"Not yet. I got us some other goodies, too." Jimmy shows her the drugs from his pocket.

"Wow, did you hit the lotto or something?"

"I mugged an old lady on the street. I beat the shit out of her; she might be dead."

"You better be joking!"

"Yeah, I am. I know where to get money when I need it." Jimmy says proudly. "We can start the party after we eat."

"I don't know. I kinda feel like just hanging out for today."

"Yeah, I feel like shit myself. That's probably a good idea."

Jimmy and Osana settle into a comforting sense of stillness, opting for a cozy day in. Osana's idea of a perfect time was a marathon of cheap horror movies, and Jimmy is fine with it. Although his mental state continues to degenerate into murkier and gloomier affairs. He knows he needs to keep these thoughts to himself and pretends to appear as his usual self.

The next couple of days unfold in much the same way. They spend hours lounging around, eating, sex, and the occasional dip into the drug stash, mostly on Jimmy's part. They even prepare a simple dinner together one night. Osana enjoys cooking, and they work in silence, occasionally exchanging smiles and glances. Osana does catch Jimmy lightly jabbing a kitchen knife into his forearm at one point. This appears to be a violent act but is unsure if it is directed at himself or someone else. He could just be playing with the knife, of course. In any event, she believes it is not intended for her and chooses not to mention it for fear of ruining the moment.

As they set the table, Osana mentions how peaceful the day has been. Jimmy agrees, noting these are the moments he needs the most.

The next day follows the same restful pattern. Osana gives Jimmy a few small projects to do around the apartment, which he seems to truly enjoy. As evening approaches, they decide to wind down with more movies.

As the weekend comes to a close, they are feeling much better and full of energy. Jimmy realizes his stash is running low, so his mind turns to scoring more drugs. He does not want to bring it up to Osana directly, choosing another approach. "We've been cooped up in here long enough. How 'bout we go grab some pizza?"

"Sounds good. I'll get Amy ready."

"Um, let's see if Elvie or Bella's available to watch her, no?"

"Ok, fine with me." Osana makes a couple of calls and Bella is available.

A t the local pizzeria, Jimmy and Osana finish their slices and beers. Jimmy sees Osana is as drunk as he is, so he sets his plan in motion. "Man, those beers hit the spot, huh?" testing Osana's mindset.

"Yeah, I'm feeling pretty good. I think you ordered too many beers."

"Nah, we're having a good time. Just relax." Jimmy pretends to read his empty bottle of beer for a moment then looks up. "Hey, maybe we should go see Spark on the way home?"

"I won't complain!"

The urge to get high has come upon them. Jimmy still has money from his credit card cash advance and is ready for a night of recklessness. Osana calls Bella as they leave the pizzeria to see if Amy could stay with her until later that night, which is fine with Bella.

They stagger two blocks out of their way and find Spark in one of his spots. Meth and cocaine are available and Jimmy, flush with cash, gets carried away with the amounts. So much so Osana tugs on his sleeve to reel him in. By this time, they already have enough drugs to keep them thoroughly stoned for more than a couple of days. It is time to head to Osana's.

At Osana's the time is grinding on and the drugs have taken hold. They start with the cannabis vape pen and cocaine, which puts them in a wild disposition. Osana puts on music, but it is too loud for Jimmy, worried one of the neighbors might call the police, so Osana lowers it. This does not stop Osana from dancing seductively around Jimmy.

Osana is soon back on the couch with Jimmy where they kiss and fondle each other. They only take short breaks to boost their highs. The night continues in a blur of highs and lows. The drugs shift from weed and coke to meth for a more intense high.

The apartment is a flurry of frenzied energy and excited laughter, punctuated by moments of drug-induced deep paranoia. The outside world encroaches upon them as the distant sounds of sirens and shouting on the street seem to creep closer with each passing hour. The meth is causing Jimmy to panic over every little 'strange noise' he hears.

By daybreak, Osana is sitting in the kitchen, staring at the peeling wallpaper with a look of hollow meditation. Jimmy, his face haggard and eyes glassy, is pacing back and forth, talking to himself about how they need to leave before 'they' get there. He has no sense of time, only the relentless need for more drugs and alcohol.

Osana's phone rings. The two of them are instantly torn out of their daydreams and brought back to some semblance of reality. Osana looks at her phone and sees it is Bella, she picks up. "Yeah Bella, what's up?"

"You forgot you got a baby over here?"

"No, no. Umm, can I get her in a while? Just let me straighten up."

"Yeah, that's fine. I got nothing to do until later."

As Osana gets off the phone Jimmy questions her about it. "Who was that?"

"It was Bella. She wants me to get Amy."

"You sure it was her? You know they have devices that can copy anybody's voice now."

"Yes, Jimmy. I know it was her." Osana says mockingly. "I may be stoned, but I know my friends."

"Ok, we gotta be careful, ya know. That door could bust in any second."

"Whatever you say, babe. I gonna take a shower and go get her."

Jimmy nods and goes back to the couch and puts the television on, but just keeps surfing through the channels until he starts nodding off and on.

When Osana is ready she tells Jimmy she will be back soon with Amy. Jimmy mumbles some words in agreement.

Osana makes her way over to Bella's wearing a baseball cap and sunglasses just in case she runs into anyone, specifically law enforcement. She cautiously reaches Bella's apartment and as they pack up the baby's things, they get into a conversation Osana does not want to have. Especially when Bella starts to ask what she and Jimmy have been doing; Osana tries to downplay the events. "Nothing really, just hanging out together. Doing a little bit of this and that."

"Oh, don't bullshit me, Osana. Look at you! You've been hitting it hard all night. Did you even sleep?"

"Yeah, I slept. Everything's cool. Quit bugging me about it."

"I bet Jimmy's still there all fucked up, ain't he?"

"I think he's sleeping now, we ain't done shit for hours." Osana feels bad about having to lie to her best friend.

"Osana, c'mon, why you holding back?"

"Ugh ok, things got a little out of hand and went on too long... but mostly him. He got more fucked up than usual, acting weird and shit."

"Like what?"

"Just shit he was saying how fucked up his life is, it's all bullshit anyway, people will learn one day, shit like that."

"Wow, what the fuck does that mean?"

"Who knows. He's just bugging." Osana is bothered by Jimmy's behavior but does not to alarm her friend. It would be embarrassing if Bella knew Osana has lost control over the situation.

"You stash any for yourself?"

"Of course, I put a bunch of shit in my secret spot!"

"All right, girl! Good for you."

"Hey, we know how to take care of ourselves." Osana says as she leaves. She returns home and spends time caring for Amy. Jimmy is fully passed out in the living room, which Osana is glad to see. It gives her time to focus on some other matters around the apartment.

J immy wakes from his sleep in the late afternoon and finishes off the last of the drugs. As the evening drags on, his euphoria gives way to exhaustion and despair. The apartment, once an exciting backdrop, now feels like a prison to him. The initial thrill has dissolved into a haunting sense of dread. Jimmy looks around and finds himself sitting on the floor, surrounded by empty bottles and discarded wrappers. "We got anything left? Jimmy asks self-consciously.

"There ain't nothing here. You finished the last of it. Don't tell me you want more?"

"Liar, I know you hide shit somewhere."

"What? You're nuts. You did everything." Osana acts innocently.

"Well, are you going out?"

"Me? You want it. Why do I have to go?"

"Ok, relax. Jimmy paces back and forth for a couple of minutes."

"I'm gonna go see if Spark is around. Be right back."

"Get something to eat, too." Osana insists.

"Eat? Who the fuck can eat?"

"I can."

Jimmy puts on his jacket, walks out, and begins his search for Spark. After inquiring with a few familiar faces he finds Spark sitting in his car in a parking lot. "Hey, Spark, how ya doing?"

"What's going on, my man? You look in better shape tonight."

"Thanks. I'm really sorry—"

"What do you need?"

"Same shit. Looking to get cranked up."

"Oh ok, I got what you need." Spark says going through a brown paper bag on his lap. "Ice? You got money?"

"Sure." Jimmy pulls out several folded bills from his pocket.

"Cool. I got you."

Jimmy is more panicky, but he can't tell if it's his need for drugs or the nervousness of buying drugs by himself for the first time.

Locked Up

What neither Jimmy nor Spark have any way of knowing is they are under surveillance by a New York City Police Department drug squad. As soon as the exchange is made two police cars swoop into the parking lot with lights and sirens blaring. "Nobody fuckin' move" scream the officers as they rush toward Jimmy and Spark.

Before Jimmy can even process what is happening, he finds himself pressed against one of the police cars and being placed in handcuffs. Over his shoulder he watches as Spark is yanked out of his car and thrown to the ground. Jimmy and Spark are searched thoroughly. More drugs are found in Spark's vehicle adding to his charges.

Spark seems to take this in stride, but Jimmy's mind goes numb as he is placed in the back of a separate police vehicle. He is brought to the police station, processed, and tossed into a holding cell. Jimmy is hoping Spark will be in the cell with him as support or defense, but figures he is still being questioned.

The shame and regret is overwhelming as he sits in the corner of the dimly lit cell crammed with five other detainees. The flickering light from a single fluorescent fixture is casting eerie shadows making Jimmy more uneasy than he already is.

Three of the detainees look harmless, like they are locked up for drunk driving or shoplifting. The other two look like violent offenders. They are not sitting peacefully waiting to be released, they pace back and forth like caged lions looking for their next prey. The bigger of them is a muscular man with many tattoos and a scar across his cheek. The other is a slender character with a facial tick who scans the cell with a smirk on his filthy, unshaven face. He settles on Jimmy. "Well, well, what have we here? A new face. Lookin' a bit out of place, aren't ya?"

The bigger detainee walks over to join the ridiculing. "Yeah, man. Never seen you around before. You got a name? I'm Lynch and my buddy here we call Fisheye."

Jimmy looks up, his voice trembling. "Jimmy. Just... just trying to keep to myself guys."

Fisheye takes a step closer to Jimmy "Trying to keep to yourself?" That's cute. The man is so close Jimmy smells the stale cigarettes and sweat, it is overpowering. Jimmy moves further back on the bench.

"Hey Lynch, I bet this guy went to college. What do you think?"

"Yeah, he looks like one of them fuckers. You went to Havard, right?"

"I'm just a garbage man, that's all."

"Don't bullshit me. You know what happens to punks like you in here?"

Fisheye takes another step closer. "They get picked apart. You think you're special just 'cause you're quiet? It don't work that way, bro."

Jimmy swallows hard and looks down at the floor. He is sweating profusely, his hands tremble as he grips his pant legs. He tells them again he doesn't want any trouble; he's just waiting to get out. Fisheye continues his pestering as Lynch steps closer to Jimmy. "Just waiting to get out? You gotta show some balls in here. Or maybe you're just a snitch. Are you a snitch, Jimmy? Is that your plan?"

"Maybe he wants to give up that pretty mouth." Lynch takes another step closer, his shadow looms over Jimmy. He taps a finger on Jimmy's head, making him flinch. "Guys like you gotta suck dick to stay alive in the joint, ya know."

The vision of being forced to perform such an act rushes through his mind, sending a chill down Jimmy's spine.

"No, he's a garbage man, Lynch, he wants it in the can! Fisheye says laughingly. "Get it, Lynch? Garbage man... can. Get it?"

"Yeah, I get it. Maybe you're right."

Jimmy is in full panic mode now, unsure what will happen next.

Fisheye continues. "We could use a little entertainment while we wait. You wanna entertain us, Jimbo?

"No, please. I just want to be left alone."

Lynch grabs Jimmy by the collar and yanks him to his feet. Jimmy's face grows pale, eyes wide with fear. Fisheye stands there, watching with a smirk, and warns Jimmy. "That's not how it works, mother fucker. You gotta show you're tough. Or at least, not act like a fuckin' pussy scared outta your mind."

Lynch slams Jimmy back on the bench causing Jimmy to strike his head forcefully against the concrete wall. It hurt Jimmy considerably, but he dares not show it to these guys.

Fisheye leans into Jimmy. "Guess he's not up for it. Fuckin' guy is boring me now."

Lynch adds "Yeah, he's no fuckin' fun this guy." As they move back to the other side of the cell exchanging more vulgarities about Jimmy.

Their laughter begins to fade into the background as Jimmy's mind withdraws into thoughts about what he has become. He resolves to keep his eyes fixed on the floor until he can get himself out of the awful hellhole.

The next couple of days are a blur of court, transfers, judges, and paperwork; none of which he is familiar with. Jimmy's world is collapsing around him, and he has no idea how he is going to explain this to Osana or Marie. His family and friends are going to be shocked and disappointed with him.

He is charged with attempted possession of a controlled substance, an offense that could carry a long prison sentence. However, his assigned public defender negotiates a deal that includes mandatory counseling and rehabilitation instead of jail time. Fortunately for Jimmy, the judge recognizes he is a first offender who has made a critical mistake.

Once released Jimmy stands outside the building choosing which way he should go – home to Marie or back to Osana's. He believes he will receive more comfort from Marie, so he heads there.

҈҈҈

He is terrified as he walks into the apartment, knowing this is going to the argument to make all others pale in comparison.

Marie is stunned to see him. "What are you doing here?! I should have changed that stupid lock."

"Marie... Marie... I know. I'm sorry, but I got into some trouble."

"You left us, remember? Why should I give a shit!" Marie blurts out. "What trouble are you in? Tell me!" Marie waits for an answer as Jimmy stands there with his head down. She can tell this is no ordinary mess he is in. "Well?! What happened? You were with that whore?"

After a few seconds, Jimmy comes out with it. "I was arrest-ed."

"What?! Are you crazy?" Marie screams hysterically.

"Easy Marie, I really need help now."

"What were you arrested for?"

"Buying drugs, I guess."

"Oh my god! You guess? What are you even talking about?"

"I was with a friend—"

"A friend?"

"And they wanted to get some drugs, so I went out to try and buy some."

"Are you an idiot? I don't even know what to say. This is the way you come back? So, you're going to jail?"

"No, the lawyer they gave me got me a good deal, so I don't have to. I gotta do some other stuff though, counseling and shit."

"Are you going to lose your job now? We need the benefits."

"No, everything's good at work. They won't even know." Jimmy says knowing he is already on the verge of losing his job.

"You'd better be right. We can't afford this. I have to take care of Jeannie, I can't work."

"And who's this friend? A woman?"

"No, it's just a bunch of guys I know." Jimmy continues his concocted story.

"Don't bullshit me. You were in Hunts Point?"

"Yeah, around there."

"I can't believe this, Jimmy. I don't know you anymore. We're barely scraping by, and you know you have responsibil-ities. You'd better not get in more trouble. We need the money, Jimmy."

"I'm trying to keep it together, Marie. I just feel like I'm under a lot of stress."

"All you have is excuses. So, you're an addict now?"

"No, don't be crazy. It was a one-time thing, not even for me."

Tears run down Marie's face. "But buying drugs? You're going to end up destroying everything we've worked for. The bills keep coming in and you think I'm just supposed to sit here and do nothing while we sink into debt or something?"

"That's not going to happen. I'm not like one of those drug addicts." Jimmy declares denying his reality.

"You sound like one. You're starting to look like one. I can't believe you were arrested! We already have all these medical bills and you put yourself in legal trouble."

Jimmy slowly nods. "I'm going to take care of this, Marie, everything."

The two of them stand there looking at each other for a while. Jimmy knows he screwed up, but thinks Marie is worried about money, not him.

"I haven't slept in two days, Marie. I gotta lay down for a while."

"You think I'm going to let you stay here?"

"Please, Marie. I'm in bad shape."

"I know you are. Look at you!" Jimmy looks so pitiful begging for compassion it hurts her heart. "Go ahead. You do whatever you want now anyway."

"Where are the kids?"

"Bobby's at school and Jeannie's taking a nap in the crib. So be quiet."

"Yeah, I know, I will." Jimmy says in a defeated tone.

Jimmy walks slowly to the bedroom, undresses, and sits on the edge of the bed. Marie comes in a short while later. "You're not going to take a shower after being in that dirty place?"

"I am. Just thinking a bit." He gets up, showers, and gets to bed. He falls asleep almost immediately after the chaos he's been through, briefly wondering what Osana is thinking about him not returning.

Marie picks up her phone to call Gina but is too embarrassed to go through with it. She can't help but speculate on what this means for the future but cannot seem to think clearly. She realizes she needs to seek advice from someone, so she decides to call her mother, Nancy. The phone rings three times, but, thankfully, her mother answers. "Hi honey. I was just thinking of calling you."

Marie's voice cracks. "Mom... I... I don't know what to do. Jimmy... he's been arrested."

There is a pause at the other end that seems to last for a very long time, then a worried exhale. "What happened? Is he okay?"

"I don't know, Mom," Marie whispers, tears ready to spill over. "He's here now, sleeping. He said he got caught buying drugs for friends, but I know there's a woman involved. I just... I don't understand. I don't know where this comes from. How could he do this? I don't know who he is anymore."

"Another woman? What else is going on?"

"I didn't want to trouble you, but we're separated now. He stays with some woman up in Hunts Point, I think."

"Why haven't you called me? Oh, Marie, I feel so bad. You shouldn't be going through something like that alone. I'm your mother."

"I know mom, I'm sorry. I guess I was trying to deny it was happening."

Her mother's voice is steady, but Marie can hear the concern beneath it. "Sweetheart, this must all be very upsetting but try to stay calm. We'll figure this out together. I'm always here for you, okay?"

Marie squeezes her eyes shut, trying to steady herself. "I don't know what to do, Mom. I'm afraid. Everything is changing. I don't want to give up, but I don't know how to help him. I don't even know where to start."

"Honey, listen to me. Sometimes people make choices we don't understand, even hurt us, but we have to think clearly. You're in shock right now, and that's completely normal. We need to take things one step at a time."

"I wish dad was still here." Marie says softly.

"Me, too. I know you miss him as much as I do." Nancy's sadness is obvious, but brings herself back to the problem at hand. "What has he told you about the arrest?"

"Nothing yet. He said he was up for two days in jail and wanted to sleep. But what if there's more to this than I realize? What if there is more he's been hiding? Marie chokes on her words, the weight of the unknown crashes down on her.

"Sweetheart, we can't know what's going on in his mind, but I can tell you, no matter what you're feeling right now, he's still your husband. We need to make sure he gets help, and you need to take care of yourself, too."

Marie lets her mother's words sink in. "I don't know if I can do this, Mom. I feel so lost."

"I will help you. I'll make some calls and we'll find a lawyer. We'll figure out what happened and a way to protect you and the kids. But you need to take it one step at a time. Let's focus on what we can do tonight. Tomorrow will be a new day, and we'll have a plan."

Marie wipes her eyes, feeling a glimmer of encouragement in her mother's words, though it isn't enough to quiet the panic in her chest. "Ok, I'll try. But, mom I don't know where this ends."

"I know, sweetie. I know. But whatever happens, I'm here. We'll figure it out, I promise."

"Thanks, Mom. I just... I don't what's happened to my life."

"You start by taking care of yourself. Get some rest, and tomorrow, we'll talk tomorrow about the next steps. We're going to get through this. You said he's there now?"

"Yeah, he's sleeping."

"Ok, let him sleep, but keep a careful eye on him."

"I will, mom. I'll call you tomorrow." Marie sits back, her mother's words echo in her mind, offering comfort, but the knot in her stomach remains. Her life has been forever changed again.

Jimmy awakens, it is dark outside and Marie is asleep next to him. The red numbers on the digital clock next to the bed read 3:00 a.m. "Holy shit", he mutters, "I've been asleep for 15 hours?" He gets up, eats something out of the refrigerator, and goes back to bed.

The Counseling Session

The next few days are tense with Marie barely speaking to Jimmy. On the third morning, he tells Marie he is going to his first counseling session, and he should be back in a couple of hours. She barely responds as Jimmy heads out of the door.

Jimmy arrives outside the small, nondescript office building, and stands there for a few minutes gathering his composure. The gray concrete façade and dreary signage seem foreboding, although he should not have expected anything else. This is only his first step in satisfying the court's mandates, but it feels like the end of the line to him.

Eventually making it inside, Jimmy's hands are sweaty and his fingers are wrapped tightly around the worn armrests of the waiting room chair.

Inside, the space is like a movie set more than real life. The waiting area is painted a soothing green, festooned with posters and placards of various affirmations. The room smells of some sort of disinfectant interfering with his already erratic mental state.

His appointed counselor, a middle-aged woman dressed in a cheap nylon outfit with scrutinizing eyes and a pretend smile, enters the waiting room from a door to his right. "Hi, I'm Sandra. You must be Jimmy."

Jimmy stands up quickly and replies "Hello. Yeah, that's me."

"Come on in. Let's get started," Sandra says, gesturing to the room.

Inside, the room appears comfortable with chairs arranged in a half circle. There is a small table in the center with a box of tissues, a pitcher of water and a stack of plastic cups. Sandra settles into one of the chairs and motions Jimmy to take a seat across from her.

"So, I'm glad you're here today," Sandra begins. Her voice is calm and steady but does nothing to ease Jimmy's apprehension. "I know you are mandated to attend these sessions, but how are you feeling about starting this process?"

Jimmy takes some time to respond. "I'm... I'm worried. I don't really know what to expect. I know what I did, I'm not sure I belong here, though."

Sandra shakes her head sympathetically. "It's normal to feel anxious. This is a big step, and it's okay to take it one moment at a time. How about we start by talking a little about what brought you here?"

Jimmy is reluctant. The words are somewhere in his head but letting them out feels like it would open the flow gates, and he is not sure he is ready for that.

After a while of no response, Sandra breaks the silence with procedural matters and reassurances regarding privacy. Jimmy starts to feel like he could mention some of the more basic realities of his life. But the clock on the wall is ticking louder than his thoughts, each tick a reminder of the weight he carries. He is still convinced he can handle everything on his own.

"So, would you like to talk about what brought you here?" Sandra proposes, adjusting herself in the chair.

Jimmy, sweat forming on his forehead. "I... I guess I just got carried away. I don't even remember the last couple of days before I got arrested."

"You were using for those days?"

Jimmy swallows hard. "Yeah, I was. I never even really drank or smoked, but I just got sucked into it. I just felt like it."

"Are these feelings all a recent development?" Sandra scribbles a few notes.

"Well, to be honest I think it's something that's been going on for a long time. I get sad a lot, but I always feel empty inside; not sure how to describe it."

"I see. It sounds like this has been going on your whole life."

"I guess. I really can't remember when I didn't feel like this." Jimmy opens up honestly.

"So, you sought out drugs as a way to self-medicate?"

"If this didn't happen, I probably would have never done drugs."

"So, what is the 'this' you mentioned? The catalyst that brought you to drugs."

"I met a woman who makes me feel alive for once."

"And she's a drug user?"

"Yes. I only did it a few times with her, but it's sunk into something I can't control."

"It sounds like it was more than a few times, wasn't it Jimmy?"

"Yeah, you're right. I just want to stop feeling the way I do. It's draining. I don't know if you can understand."

"How are the other parts of your life?"

"Everything seems to be suffering, my relationship with my wife and kids, my job's at risk, and I feel bad about myself. I was trying to feel better, but I'm going to lose everything now."

"It sounds like you have a lot on your shoulders. But you don't have to carry it alone anymore. It's okay to lean on me and on others who are going through similar struggles."

Sandra and Jimmy talk about many things for the rest of the time. Jimmy even shares stories of his past which help Sandra gain insight into his current behaviors.

"I had a fight at school one day... more like a kid punched me in the eye for some stupid shirt I had on. It hurt a lot. My mother put ice on it when I got home, but she was kind of blaming me for it." Anger starts to show through as Jimmy speaks. "Then my fucking father comes home, and he barely looks at it. He told me it'll go away in a few days, no big deal. I mean, what the fuck is that?"

"I can see how that would leave a lasting impression on you, Jimmy." Sandra says supportively.

"Yeah, and I had trouble with girlfriends, looking for work and all sorts of shit – and I never got one fucking hint of support or advice or anything, so I shut the fuck up. It's better to just keep everything inside."

"You say you had trouble with girlfriends. What was that like?"

"I could meet them pretty easy, but I never could seem to get more than one date. I'd try to do my best, take them to nice places and all, but it never worked out."

Sandra can see Jimmy is suffering from hopelessness and depression. She knows she needs to develop a plan of action and they will need several sessions to dig into everything he has been dealing with.

By the end of the session, Jimmy is experiencing a mixture of annoyance and exhaustion, but not hope. As he walks to his car, his mind begins to devalue the session and Sandra's motives for listening to him. "Who does she think she's kidding; she don't give a shit! As long as people keep getting arrested and sent to her bullshit office, she'll keep making money. And I told her shit, what a fucking idiot. Fuck her!"

He decides to sit in the park across the street for a while to try and cool off. The park is serene, with the distant sound of children playing. Yet Jimmy finds himself drawn to the shadows of the trees. He sits on a bench and replays every word from the session. He is drowning in his own mistakes, and her asking him questions seems both frustrating and confusing.

As he sits, he begins to feel a loathing with the very concept of therapy. Therapy is supposed to provide clear solutions, or at least a roadmap for moving forward. Instead, this would be spinning his wheels, trapping him in a vortex of introspection that will lead nowhere, he reasons.

In his frustration, he considers abandoning therapy altogether. Maybe he needs to find answers in a different way, through action, rather than contemplation. In the coming days, Jimmy finds himself at home oscillating between anger and despair.

Life With Jimmy

Alone and bored in her apartment, Osana calls Bella to get coffee so herself and Amy can out of the apartment for a while. About an hour later they all meet them at the neighborhood café and get situated inside.

The afternoon sun filters through the large windows of the cafe, casting a warm hue over the space. The hum of conversation and the clink of coffee cups create a soothing environment. They pick a table near the window, with Bella dominating the conversation in her usual animated way. Osana listens attentively and tends to Amy in the stroller.

After a while, Bella's energy level begins to drop and the conversation becomes softer and more meaningful. Osana turns the conversation in the direction she would like it to go. "So, when are you going to meet a guy and settle down?" She asks as she searches for something in Amy's baby bag.

"You talking to me? You got a long wait for that, baby. I'm having too much fun." As soon as Bella says this, she realizes those words may upset Osana. "I mean, there's nothing wrong with wanting that, it's just ain't for me right now. I know someday I'll want it."

"It's ok, Bella. You're just being honest... as usual."

"Well, what about you? How's it going with Jimmy?"

"Jimmy? I'm not even sure where he is. He went out days ago and I haven't seen him since."

"Really? That's weird."

"Yeah, I don't know. He's probably going back and forth with his wife. He has a sick kid, like an infant."

"Oh really? What's the matter?"

"She has some kind of heart trouble. He doesn't talk about it."

"What about Carlo? You ever hear from him?"

"No, and I've kept the same number, so if he doesn't call it ain't my fault."

"That's a shame. I know you two were really in love."

"Well, things change sometimes, ya know. I'm just not lucky at love." Osana says half-jokingly.

"Oh, what have we here? Pretending you don't care?"

"You're gonna make fun of me, but I've been thinking about Jimmy more lately."

"That guy?! He's not your type at all."

"Yeah, maybe that's it. He's different in a good way. We talk for a long time, and he listens to me. He seems like he's really interested in me. And he can be funny sometimes."

"Sounds serious."

"Maybe it's him, maybe I just want it to be somebody. Maybe I need to be with a man more than you do. It's just the way I am, probably."

Bella leans over the table more. "What if you start something with him, and Carlo comes back?"

"Carlo? What if he got twenty years in Texas? I don't know what's going on with him either."

"Yeah, true. There's a way to find out if you want."

"I went to see him in jail, and he wouldn't tell me anything. If he hasn't called me by now, I'm not looking for him. Let him rot wherever he is." Osana says in an annoyed tone.

"Oh wow. It sounds like somebody's in love with two guys!"

"Shut up you!" Osana says in a more positive voice. "I'm just lonely, I guess. It's been a while since I felt this way, or anyway, about a man." Osana considers the longing to be loved is what she and Jimmy have in common.

"So, it ain't just about the money?"

"Oh, I still need that! I got my needs, right?"

"I hear that! Can't it be both? I mean what the hell!" Bella exclaims.

"Yeah, it's gonna have to be both for a while. I ain't sure about him, but I'm sure I gotta get my buzz on."

"I know, it's rough, Osana. These friggin' guys have no idea what we women go through. They got it easy. All they do is worry about putting their tiny dicks somewhere... anywhere."

"I know, but it doesn't make it any easier sometimes." Osana squeezes Bella's hand in gratitude. She looks out the window, lost in thought, her mind swirling with the possibilities of what she should do next. "Thanks for coming out today, Bella."

Bella grins and gestures knowingly.

❦❦❦

Osana sits at home thinking about her life since meeting Jimmy. She promised herself this new home would be her sanctuary, a place to build a better life for her daughter. That path has been compromised since meeting Jimmy. She vows to get it back on track and, after much soul searching, realizes separating from Jimmy needs to be the first step. She decides to invite him to lunch to explain her position, so she calls. Jimmy sees it is Osana calling and goes into a back room to answer away from Marie.

"Hey, babe. What are you doing?" Osana says in a pleasant voice.

"I guess not much right now. Why? What's going on?" Jimmy almost whispering.

"I was thinking about having lunch, so, ya know, if you want to come by we can eat together."

"All right, that sounds good. Am I bringing the food?"

"No, babe. I'll pick something up before you get here. It's my treat today."

"Oh cool. Ok, give me a bit and I'll be there."

"Perfect. See you soon."

The Bronx Zoo

O sana runs out and picks up food at a local restaurant and prepares the kitchen table for lunch. She is nervous as she waits but knows this needs to be done. Jimmy arrives not long after and they begin to eat.

As Jimmy eats, he notices Osana has a troubled look on her face and is not acting as her usual self. "Hey, babe, is everything ok?"

Sheepishly she says. "Yeah, I guess I should rip the band-aid off.

"Band-aid? What are you talking about?"

"I need to say something to you."

Jimmy's expression shifts from concern to confusion. "What's going on? You're scaring me."

"Jimmy, I've been thinking a lot about you and me lately. About what we're doing here."

Jimmy's brow creases. "You're not thinking about breaking up, are you?"

Osana gathers her strength. "I... I think maybe we're not a good combination. Both of us get the other one going down a bad road."

Jimmy's face gets red as the anger rises in him. "What are you talking about? You wanna trash everything we have?"

"I feel like I'm dragging you down. I have so many issues, and it's not fair to you. You had a good life, without all this drama." Osana fakes being at fault to soften the news.

"Why would you say that? I don't give a shit about the drinking and stuff. I like being here with you."

"There's too much confusion going on. I want you to be happy, Jimmy, and I don't think I can give you that."

"So, you want me to leave?"

"I don't, but—"

"Good, because I don't want to leave. I want to stay here with you."

"I think that's the problem. You like it here because you can get away with shit you couldn't do at home and it's not good."

"Ok, I get it. You think you're making me do stuff I don't want to do, but you're wrong. I want to do this."

"You're making me do it, too though. I'm supposed to be doing better. I have a baby to think of."

"So now I'm fuckin' up your life? Is that what you're really saying?"

"Jimmy, I just think the two of us together bring out the fucked up side of each other, that's all."

"What? I thought we were having fun."

"Maybe too much fun. And it's just you most of the time, it's you having fun and me cleaning up your mess!"

"Are you going to quit the other shit you do here?" Jimmy throws out referring to the tricks she has over occasionally.

"What other shit?" Osana knows what he means, but dares him to answer.

Jimmy discerns this topic is off-limits and bringing it up would mean losing the conversation. He doesn't want to lose Osana, so he backs off. "So, if we took the partying down a few notches, we'd be doing better?"

Osana is not fully comfortable with the situation, but a good starting point given Jimmy's attitude. "I think that'll be great. Can you do it?"

"Yeah, if it means that much to you, I will."

"We can give it a try, but we really have to do it." Osana concedes knowing the arrangement is destined to fail.

"We will, I promise. I'm going to show you, you'll see."

The rest of the day and evening are quiet as they share each other's company, mostly with small talk, until falling asleep on the couch.

ᕯᕯᕯ

J immy is awakened by his cell phone vibrating on the small table next to him. He pays no attention to it knowing it is Marie wondering where he is. He chooses to go ahead with his plan for the day and wakes Osana up.

"Babe, wake up!"

"What... what happened?" Osana mutters sleepily.

"Why don't we bring the baby to the zoo?" Jimmy walks over to the window. "It looks like a great day for it." It is a bright morning without a cloud in the sky. "C'mon Mommy, get ready!"

"The zoo?! What gave you that idea?" Osana is puzzled by his suggestion.

"Nothing. We're just always in this apartment. Let's get outside for once."

"I'm kinda tired. While you were sleeping I was up and down taking care of Amy all night."

"Oh c'mon. It'll be good. We'll just go for a little while and come right back."

"Well, I guess you're right." Osana reluctantly gets up, feeds the baby, and prepares a quick breakfast for her and Jimmy.

Jimmy questions Osana. "You ever been to the Bronx Zoo? It's like really close."

Osana says she walked near there once, and it took too long.

Jimmy comes out with "We ain't walking today, we'll grab a ride. It's only 10 minutes like that."

Osana and Jimmy freshen up in the bedroom when Osana asks Jimmy if he has money to do this today.

"Yeah, don't worry. I got enough right here," as he slaps the front right side of his pants.

"Yeah, well don't spend it all over there. Save some for later."

Jimmy knows exactly what she is talking about and is way ahead of her. She wants to be sure they will be able to get high that night without any issues – and so does he. He mocks her. "Oh now, it's save some for later, huh? What happened to take it easy?"

Osana realizes what she has said and tries to play it off lightheartedly. "I said take it easy, not stop."

"I got you now." he says with a smirk. "Ok, that's fine with me. Let's get going."

They make it out of the apartment without much trouble. They catch a livery cab at the corner and soon reach the entrance of the zoo on Southern Boulevard. Jimmy is happy to see a short line to get in. Even baby Amy seems excited to be there, bouncing up and down in her stroller.

The air is full of the sounds of chirping birds and distant animal calls. They wander through the pathways as Jimmy shows Amy every animal. Jimmy finds it quite interesting, too. However, Osana seems to consider this entire outing an inconvenience.

"Do you have to walk through everything? How many dirty animals you gotta see?" Osana wisecracks.

Jimmy, thinking of Amy, tries to divert Amy's attention away from her mother's negativity by walking ahead. He brings Amy over to more exhibits and reads all the signs to her. While Amy is captivated by the monkey house, Jimmy leans into Osana. "C'mon, let her have some fun. She's enjoying this."

"She doesn't even know what she's looking at! I didn't want to even come here."

"Listen, you do whatever you want all the time; give her some consideration once in a while." Jimmy speaks sharply to her.

Just as those words are leaving his mouth Jimmy realizes he has never even done this for his children. A sadness comes over him as he thinks to himself "What a piece of shit I am. What the fuck am I doing here? This isn't my family. Amy's not my child." Jimmy has misgivings for not doing the same for his family but views them as in his past at the same time.

After spending a good amount of time viewing the animals, Osana says she is hungry, so they find the nearest concession stand and have a snack. In between bites Jimmy is becoming more downhearted.

As soon as they have taken their last bites Osana starts in on how they should get back home. Jimmy truly wants to leave but feels bad for Amy, so he talks Osana into staying just a little bit more. He rushes Amy through several more exhibits, including the giraffes, the zebras, and birds. He is trying to strike some sort of balance between Amy seeing as much as possible and Osana wanting to get the hell out of there. When Jimmy figures Amy has seen enough, he concedes it is time to go home. They walk back out to Southern Boulevard and hail another livery driver.

In the cab, Amy drifts off to sleep in Osana's arms, clutching the plush monkey Jimmy had bought her. Jimmy points to Amy sleeping in her arms. "C'mon, you can't tell me you don't love that?"

Osana turns and gives him a callous sideways look and puts her head back down. Jimmy slumps back into his seat. Once back at the apartment everyone settles in, gets cleaned up, and rests from the day's activities.

Fat Lou

As Jimmy lay in Osana's bed, his mind is a jumble as he checks all the missed calls from Marie. Surely, she thinks he is out drinking and drugging again. That is not the case this time, but what Marie has in her head is irrelevant to Jimmy at this point.

He turns to look at Osana beside him, her eyes softly closed in peaceful slumber. He envies her serenity. The room is lit by the soft glow of filtered sunshine that does nothing to soothe the storm inside his head. He should have been thinking of what a good time they had but has already forgotten it.

Jimmy finds himself sinking further into the whirlpool of his thoughts, he knows his life is a mess. The failure gnaws at him, making him suffocated by invisible chains.

He tries to focus on Osana, on the warmth of her tanned skin, on the soft kisses she has given him but finds no relief. He feels pressure mounting, not just emotionally but physically. Not long ago he joked about weight loss making his pants loose, but the decline is no longer amusing. The body aches, the dark circles under his eyes, and an unshakable hacking cough are only part of his concerns. Jimmy realizes he has become increasingly depressed and paranoid and struggles to focus on minor tasks. The sense of hopelessness is constant, intensifying his drinking and drug use. He thinks of the day Osana asked him to shower because of his poor hygiene.

Osana stirs, sensing his discomfort; she looks at him with concern. "Babe, are you okay?" she asks, her voice tender and laced with worry.

Jimmy sighs. "Yeah, just a lot on my mind."

"Like what?" Osana asks genuinely concerned.

"Nothing. You wouldn't understand."

"Well, you can try me to see."

"I said forget it. You don't know the first thing about what's going through my head. Just forget it!" Jimmy snaps at her.

"Be miserable by yourself then, fuck it." Osana reacts rolling over.

He decides to get up and go out into the streets looking to buy drugs. He knows Spark is still locked up but imagines he will find another source without much trouble. After walking the nearby blocks a few times, he sees someone he knows to be a drug user by face, and that is enough for Jimmy to begin a conversation. "Hey, my friend! How ya been?"

"Good, bro. How 'bout you?"

"Yeah, same shit, ya know. Anybody doing business out here?" Jimmy inquires.

"Ya know Spark got locked up, right?"

"I know, I was with him!"

"Oh shit man, that was you?!"

"Yep. My first so I got out. Spark's a regular, I guess."

"Oh, Spark? Yeah, he's in and out. So, you cool?"

"Yeah, I've been around."

"Cool, cool. Why don't you go by the park and look for Fat Lou."

"Yeah, I'll do that. Thanks, man." With that Jimmy walks to the park to meet his new connection. This park is mostly concrete, no more than a basketball court, a few small trees, and hard benches. Upon reaching the fringes of the park he stops and scans the park's occupants.

A heavy-set man sitting near the entrance gives Jimmy a knowing nod of his head, and Jimmy walks over to him. "Lou?" Jimmy says, not daring to refer to him as 'Fat Lou.'

"Yeah, who the fuck are you?"

"I was told to look for you since Spark ain't around."

"So, you know Spark?"

"Yeah, I was with him when he got busted."

"You were with Spark that night?"

"Yeah, it was fucked up."

Fat Lou eyes Jimmy up and down. "I knew you were the guy. If I didn't, I wouldn't even be talking to you right now."

"News travels, huh?"

"Ain't shit happen around here we don't know about! One of my guys was across the street when the shit went down." Fat Lou says smugly.

"Ok, cool." Jimmy is glad to hear he will not have an issue buying.

"What you need?"

"You got any blow?'

"Nah, man. I got rocks, though."

Jimmy says, "That'll work." and hands Fat Lou some cash. Lou counts it out and hands Jimmy several vials of crack.

"I thought you'd be buying bigger than that."

"What makes you think that?"

"Look at you, man. You ain't from around here."

"Oh, yeah, I get it. I'm just kind of short."

"So, who you hanging with over here?"

"I'm staying with some woman. She lives a few blocks over."

"Maybe I know her. Who is it?"

"Her name's Osana. You probably don't know her."

"Oh shit! Osana? With the little baby Amy?"

"Yeah, yeah, That's her."

"Man, c'mon. She's a regular. I know her for years. So, you guys are pretty tight." Fat Lou's comfort level increases hearing this.

"I guess you can say that, yeah."

"You look like you can be trusted. Can you?"

"Yeah, I don't fuck around. Why?"

"Listen, I want to help you out and you can help me, too."

"What are we talking about?"

"I ain't got time to be sitting out here doing this shit. I got bigger things to do. I can use a guy like you to deal for us, at least 'til Spark gets back."

"When do you think that is?"

"With Spark's record? That fucker might get life!" Fat Lou says as a joke.

Jimmy laughs, standing with his head down thinking about Fat Lou's proposition. He is wavering between the money, drugs, and the risk he would be taking. The desire for money and drugs is outweighing his other considerations.

"You'd make real good money."

"Fuck, I can do it. What do you need from me?"

"Meet me at the barber shop over there every day at noon. I'll give you a bag and you give me the money at night. Cool?

"Yeah man, thanks. I can use the money." Jimmy walks away hoping he has not made another huge mistake but tries to focus on the present. Jimmy is thrilled to bring Osana the good news, so he stops by a liquor store before returning to her place. "Hey, babe. I'm back."

Osana is sitting on the couch and barely turns her head to acknowledge him.

"I got some goodies and some news for you."

Hearing this attracts her attention. "Really? Like what?"

Jimmy walks over, hands her the drugs, and shows her a bottle of tequila.

"Ah, tequila! Nice, I haven't had this for a long time. So, what's the news?"

Jimmy fills her in on his meeting with Fat Lou and how he is going to start dealing.

Osana reluctantly says. "I remember Lou, he's ok. We used to go buy from him once in a while."

"Once in a while...?" Jimmy says razzing her.

"Ha, very funny. He's going to trust you to sell for him?"

"Yeah, he knows I got busted with Spark and knows you, so I guess he thinks I'm ok. Do you think he's all right to do shit for?"

"Be careful with those guys, they don't give a shit about anything. Life is cheap to them. But, yeah, just to pick up some money I guess it's ok." Osana knows these are unstable and dangerous folks but wants the money Jimmy can earn. She has little hope of getting anything else useful from Jimmy being around.

"Ok cool. Let's see how it works out. How 'bout doing a few hits?"

"Not now, babe. I gotta feed Amy and get her ready to sleep. You can go in the bedroom, though."

Jimmy understands and walks away.

As Osana is feeding Amy a dinner of pureed beef mixed with sweet potato her phone rings. 'Unknown Caller' is on the screen. She thinks it is probably a telemarketer, but something tells her to answer. "Hello?" she says with an unsure voice.

"Hello, this is a collect call from Carlo, will you accept the charges? The automated voice informs her.

She peers towards the bedroom and figures Jimmy is absorbed in his activities. Her heart skips a beat with excitement. "Yes, I'll accept the charges."

The line crackles, and she hears a familiar voice. "Hey, babe," comes a deep voice on the other end. It is as if time folded back.

"Carlo?" She steadies herself against the table. "Is it really you?" Osana catches herself speaking too loudly and lowers her voice.

"Yeah, babe, who else would call you?" a touch of laughter in his voice. "I'm sorry it took me so long to call, but you know how they had me down here."

Osana has imagined this moment countless times, but now it is real, words seem inadequate. "I didn't think—" she starts, then swallows hard. "I was starting to think I'd never hear from you."

Carlo's voice softens. "I didn't want to surprise you like this. I just got released and I'm taking care of a few things before I come home."

Her heart aches at the word 'home,' evoking visions of a life full of dreams before it all unraveled. "What do you mean 'taking care of things'? Can't you just come home?" she asks, her voice trembling with apprehension.

"There's some final shit I gotta handle with court, and some shit I gotta do with my boys first" Carlo explains. "But I promise, then I'll be back on track. I'll be on my way soon."

Osana closes her eyes, trying to imagine the logistics of his return. "I—I'm really glad you called," she manages to say. "I've missed you so much."

"I love you and miss you too. How's my little baby doing?" Carlo asks her, his voice earnest.

"She's doing fine, getting big already. And she eats a lot like her mother!" Osana laughs.

"I'll see her very soon, my love. I know I've got a lot to make up for. But I'm ready to try to rebuild what we had."

Tears well up in Osana's eyes. She wipes them away, trying to steady her voice. "I'm here. I want you here, too."

Osana takes a deep breath, her mind floods with emotions. She has waited so long for this call and hopes it will bring a semblance of peace to her life.

"I'll wait for you," she says. "I'll start getting things ready here. Don't get arrested again, you dumb shit!" Osana says lightheartedly.

Carlo laughs, his relief is palpable through the phone. "Thank you, babe. That means more to me than you know. I'll call you again to tell you where I am."

"Okay," Osana utters softly. "I need you here. Hurry."

"I know. Thank you, babe."

They exchange a few more words, each one laced with the tentative hope of rebuilding their lives together. As Osana hangs up the phone, she looks at Amy in her highchair. "Daddy's coming home, baby." For the first time in months, Osana feels a flutter of excitement and anxiety knitting in her chest.

But what to do about Jimmy is the question. She does have some feelings for him, but nothing like what she feels for Carlo. Jimmy will have to get out of her life completely and, given his increasingly unstable state, she is not sure how he is going to take the news. She will wait until the time was right to tell him.

First Day Dealing

While out doing some errands Jimmy chooses to drive by the apartment building where Marie and the kids live. Not to see his family, but to try and process thoughts of remorse that creep into his thoughts from time to time.

He parks across the street and sits alone in his car. The engine is off, and the only sound is the hum of street traffic. Jimmy stares through the windshield; his gaze fixed on the brick apartment building that was once the center of his world. It already feels like a relic of another life, a life that seems both distant, but intimately familiar. He wonders what Marie and the children are doing, trying to figure out how he feels about leaving them.

He exhales, not knowing if he should feel regret or contentment, but knows he failed them either way. It is an odd mix of feelings, realizing the past is irrevocably gone but not knowing what to do with the memories. He takes one last look at the house, starts the car, and drives away. He arrives back at Osana's in a dark mood. She detects this is not the time to bring up Carlo's arrival, but she is bursting with the news.

On top of all the other issues Jimmy has on his mind, it is his first day as a street-level drug dealer. He meets this with a sense of uneasy anticipation. He wonders how he has gotten so far off track from his earlier life so quickly.

He is thrust into this new, dangerous role, guided by a blend of desperation and unexpected options. He convinces himself this would only be a temporary affair just to get to the next move in his life. After a quick sandwich from the corner store, Jimmy sets off on his next venture.

"Babe, I gotta go meet Lou. I'll see you later."

"You gonna be back late?"

"Not too late, I don't think. I didn't get any specific hours from him."

"Here, take this set of keys, and don't wake us up if it's late."

"Cool. Thanks." Jimmy kisses Osana and heads out the door.

Jimmy meets Fat Lou at the appointed location to receive his orders for the day. Fat Lou is stationed in an old armchair in the back of a vacant barber shop with a small group of other people around him.

"Stay low, stay smart, and don't fuck up," Fat Lou instructs, his tone carrying serious weight to it. "You mess up, you don't just lose cash. You lose a lot more. Get me?"

Jimmy nods, the gravity of his situation sinks in as Fat Lou guides Jimmy onto the street. The area is a maze of crumbling buildings, a place where hope seems as fleeting as the trash littering the sidewalks.

"Here's your product for the day." Fat Lou says as he hands Jimmy a worn-out fanny pack filled with bags of carefully packaged drugs. "And here take this just in case you run into trouble." Fat Lou hands Jimmy an old rusted .38 caliber handgun. "You ever shot one of these?"

"Yeah, no problem, Lou. I got it." Jimmy lies to Fat Lou. He has never even held a gun in his life but knows he must play the game.

"That's what we want to hear. Ok, get to it man, and don't forget we know what's in there and how much money you gotta bring back, so don't get any funny ideas."

"You don't have to worry about me."

Jimmy settles into his designated post. His heart pounds and sweat forms on his forehead and upper lip. It would be disastrous if he gets arrested again for buying drugs, but carrying an entire fanny pack of drugs and an illegal handgun could get him locked up for many years. Jimmy is sinking deeper and deeper into a black hole of gloom.

Jimmy's job is simple: keep an eye out for trouble and handle small transactions. He forces himself to appear confident as he holds his position. He spends most of his time looking out for police cars and people who might be thinking of robbing him.

The day is an endless blur of faces—some familiar, some not. Jimmy tries to stay alert, though anxiety is making it hard to concentrate. He quickly learns the unspoken rules of the trade: the quick exchanges, the nods, the guarded glances. Most of the buyers seem indifferent, but there are moments when their eyes flicker with something bleaker. It is a mix of desperation and anger he has never witnessed or even knew existed.

Then it happens, Jimmy encounters his first real challenge. A man approaches, his clothes disheveled and an agitated demeanor. He demands drugs Jimmy does not have on him. Jimmy tries to stay calm, remembering Fat Lou's warnings. "I can't help you with that," Jimmy says, his voice steadier than he is. "You need to go somewhere else."

The man's eyes narrowed, and for a moment, Jimmy fears the situation is going to escalate. He is afraid he may have to use the handgun in his jacket pocket. But before things go too far, Fat Lou appears, his presence commanding and authoritative. "Everything alright here?" Fat Lou's voice is calm but firm. The man backs off, mumbling something about coming back tomorrow. Jimmy exhales.

As the day wears on, Jimmy becomes more adept at handling various situations. He learns to read people's body language, gauge their moods, and avoid potential conflicts. By late afternoon, he is starting to feel a sliver of competence. Maybe he can do this after all.

His shift ends with the streetlights casting long shadows across the park. Jimmy returns to the former barber shop, where he can relax somewhat. Fat Lou counts the day's earnings. "Not bad for a first day," he says, tossing Jimmy cash and a plastic bag of meth. "But remember, this is just the beginning. Tomorrow, you need to be sharper. You almost got fucked out there today by that guy."

"I know. Thanks for the help. I think the biggest problem is some people back off not knowing who I was, so I lost some business with that."

"That'll straighten itself out in a couple of days when folks learn you're with us. Don't worry."

Jimmy takes the cash, feeling a mix of relief and disquiet. The money is more than he expected, but it comes at a cost he is only beginning to understand.

Jimmy gets back to the apartment and finds Osana watching television with Amy in her arms. He walks up and throws a few twenty-dollar bills in her lap.

Osana looks up at him and smiles. "We got money?"

"Yep, and there's more where that came from!" Jimmy seems to have resigned himself to this new way of life.

"Good job, Jimmy. So, it's gonna be a good night...right?"

"Yeah, but let's do something special before, like going to get a good meal and a few drinks."

"Ok, that sounds nice. I'll see if Elvie can watch the baby."

J immy and Osana make their way up to the main road and pick one of the newer restaurants to dine at. Osana has been walking by one in particular and wants to finally try it.

The restaurant is cozy, with checkered tablecloths and soft, golden lighting. They choose a table by the window and look at the menu with excitement, ordering appetizers, soups, salads, entrees, desserts, and just about whatever caught their eye on the menu. They laugh as they order more than they can eat, delighting in the choices in front of them.

When their food arrives, it is like a feast for the senses. The flavors are bold and comforting, a stark contrast to the fast food and pizza they usually eat. Between bites, they clinked glasses of beer and complement the food.

After finishing, they wander the neighborhood arm in arm telling stories and drawing attention to spots that interest them. On the way back to the apartment Osana stops for a moment and looks at Jimmy.

"Do we need to stop by you know who?" Osana asks referring to their local drug spot.

"No, babe Lou gave me some and there's two bottles of wine in the fridge." This satisfies Osana and they continue their walk and pick up Amy.

Back in Osana's apartment, they settle on the couch and indulge in the intoxicants. Eventually falling asleep right where they sit.

❦❦❦

A s the sun rises Jimmy's phone starts ringing. It is his supervisor Mark again. Jimmy knows this cannot be good. "Hey, Mark. How are you?"

"Hello Jimmy, I'm good thanks, I'm sorry to bother you, but we gotta talk."

"About what?" Jimmy braces himself for what is about to come.

"Do you have a couple of minutes?'

"Yeah, of course. What's up?"

"I want to give you a heads-up about a letter you'll be receiving tomorrow or the next day."

"A letter for what?"

"Ya know, Danny and me have been trying to cover for you being out and all, but downtown caught on and they're going to terminate your employment."

Jimmy is stunned. He knew this was bound to happen in the back of his mind, but the reality of it is devastating. "Oh, really?" Is all he can say with his head spinning trying to figure out all the implications.

"Like I said we did all we could, but this decision was made by upper management, and that's that." Mark seems truly regretful about it.

"I get it. Thanks for doing what you could. What are the next steps?"

"The letter will give you all the details about severance, final paycheck, unused vacation days, and all that. You'll also get stuff about continuing your benefits, too."

"Does Danny know?"

"Not yet, but he will soon." Mark informs him.

"I understand. Is there anything I need to do?"

"Well, if you have any department property to return or if you have personal items here, you'll need to take care of that right away after you get the letter. Just call me and we'll set it up."

"Ok, Mark, thank you for letting me know."

"Thanks for understanding. I wish you the best and take care of whatever it is you're going through. Take care, Jimmy."

Jimmy gets off the phone visibly shaken and looks at Osana.

"Who was that? You look like you saw a ghost or something." Osana says.

"Worse, I just got fired!" Jimmy says exasperated.

"Fired? For what?"

"For being a fuck up, that's what." Hitting himself in the head.

"You can sue them, ya know."

"Shut up! You don't know what the fuck you're talking about."

"Well, fuck them. You got money coming in with Fat Lou."

"Lou don't offer health benefits! I got a sick daughter, remember?"

"But you're getting cash—"

"Another one! All you women give a shit about is money. What am I a fuckin' ATM?"

"Alright... never mind. Fuck you then." Osana hollers back.

Jimmy falls back on the couch with his head in his hands and begins crying.

"Can't you go somewhere else? I don't like that shit here."

Jimmy picks his head up and stares at her for a minute. "I know, you don't give a shit about me either." He quietly stands up and walks out of the apartment.

※※※

"I'm really fucked now." Jimmy says out loud as he sits in his car trying to figure out what his next move should be. He has screwed up both of his living arrangements and his car is now the only shelter he has left.

Jimmy has always commended himself on being a man who could handle anything life threw his way. But as he sits in the driver's seat of his sedan, he feels the stab of uncertainty. The argument with Marie was so intense it won't be smoothed over any time soon, and he is still too upset about Osana's reaction to face her.

Luckily for Jimmy, there are a few essentials in the trunk of the car left over from picnics or days at the beach – a blanket, a couple of t-shirts, and even a few bags of snacks.

The first night is the hardest with Jimmy in the backseat with a rolled-up jacket for a pillow. He stares at the ceiling of his car, his mind running through the last words Osana and Marie each said to him. The quiet of the car seems deafening, a stark contrast to the discord of his recent fights.

Jimmy quickly develops a routine. Mornings are spent at the local diner, sipping coffee and eating pancakes while reading the newspaper. Afternoons and evenings are spent working for Fat Lou when needed. He finds solace in the desolation of this existence, somehow. While trying to fall asleep one night his phone rings. The caller ID shows it is Marie. He watches it ring and decides not to answer. "Fuck it. I've had enough bullshit lately."

The Hospital Visit

Marie sits in a hospital cafeteria nervously drinking tea. As the call goes to voicemail, she thinks about the message she is about to leave, and how Jimmy is going to react.

It was a routine doctor's appointment for Jeannie turned urgent. Marie's emotions churn blending into a storm she struggles to control. Jimmy needs to know the gravity of the situation, but the resentment she feels toward him makes it hard to be civil. She takes a moment to compose herself, though the strain is evident in her voice.

"Jimmy," her tone tight with tension. "This is Marie. I'm calling because Jeannie is in the hospital." She can barely keep the tremor out of her voice. "She's... she's been admitted with an infection. It's serious. I'm scared."

The silence on the other end seems to mock her. Jimmy's name on her screen in sterile text is a barrier she cannot break through. Her fingers tighten around the phone as she fights to keep her voice steady.

"I don't know if you care," she continues, the bitterness creeping into her words. "But this isn't about us. It's about her, she needs her father. I don't want to play games or make this harder than it is. I just need you to be here."

Her voice cracks slightly as she forces out the next words, the anger and hurt mingling with desperation. "I hope you can put whatever it is between us aside and be a parent. She's our daughter, and she needs both of us."

Marie's breath hitches as she pauses, "Just...just come if you can. Please." her voice barely above a whisper. "I don't know what else to say."

She ends the call sinking back into the chair. The anger has been an armor, a way to shield herself from the fear and helplessness she feels. But now, as the message replays in her mind, she is left with a hollow feeling. She stands and moves quickly back to Jeannie's room to check on her.

Marie glances at the clock on the wall frequently. Time seems to crawl, each second stretching into an eternity. She hopes, more than anything, that Jimmy will hear her message, that he will come. But deep down, she isn't sure if hope is enough.

The hospital room is a world apart from the refuge of their home. Jeannie's tiny hand clutches hers tightly, her face pale and tired. Marie tries to offer comfort to her, but every time the door to the room opens, her heart leaps, hoping against hope Jimmy will walk through it.

The air is heavy with antiseptics and the drone of medical machines. Marie's eyes are red from lack of sleep and quiet tears. She holds Amy's hand as if trying to anchor her to this world through sheer will alone. The beeping of the heart monitor is a constant reminder of the fragility of the life it measures.

Doctors and nurses are coming in and out of the room, but Jimmy is the one she is hoping to see. After what seems like many hours Marie turns her head towards the door and sees Jimmy standing in the hallway. He seems to be frozen with guilt.

Marie looks at him, her expression a mixture of surprise and wariness. "Jimmy?" her voice catching slightly.

Jimmy steps into the room. "Marie, how is she?"

"She's holding on," Marie replies softly. "The doctors say she's getting a little better. They're trying everything they can."

Jimmy glances at the girl and his heart breaks at the sight. "Can I—can I sit with her for a while?"

"Sure, she won't wake up. They've given her something to keep her comfortable."

Jimmy takes the chair beside the bed; he gazes at his daughter's fragile form. He reaches out a trembling hand and gently touches her forehead. The gesture is tender, but the pain in Jimmy's eyes is unmistakable.

"I'm sorry," Jimmy says quietly. "I'm so sorry for everything. I know I haven't been around. I've been a terrible father, and I don't expect you to forgive me."

Marie's eyes fill with tears. "Jimmy, this isn't the time for blame. Jeannie needs us to be here, not fighting over the past."

Jimmy concedes, his throat tight. He tries to compose himself. "I just— I wish I had been there to help."

"All we can do is be here for her."

Jimmy sits in silence, watching the rhythmic rise and fall of Jeannie's small chest provides a false sense of normalcy. They sit side by side, united in their love for their child even as the separation lays heavy between them.

The room falls into a contemplative silence. For a brief moment, the past seems to dissolve, leaving behind only the present, and the shared sorrow of two parents who had once been a family. Jimmy reaches over and takes Marie's hand, his grip tentative but sincere. She looks at him, and in her eyes, there is a flicker of something—perhaps forgiveness or at least a shared understanding of their current reality.

"Thank you for coming. It means a lot."

Jimmy's own eyes misting now. "I wish it could be under better circumstances." Even in Jimmy's diminished state of mind, the seriousness of the situation moves him.

"So do I." Marie lifts her head and looks up at Jimmy. "Gina's going to be bringing Bobby here in a little while."

Jimmy's demeanor picks up hearing that. "Oh good, I want to see my boy."

"Well, Jimmy, I'd really... I mean I don't think it's a good idea for him to see you... looking like that."

Jimmy looks down at himself and realizes Marie is right. He has been wearing the same clothes for days now and he cannot think of the last time he took a proper shower or shave. Looking back up at her he sympathizes. "Yeah, I see what you mean. I'll just take off in ten minutes. I want to stay a little longer if that's ok."

"Of course, Jimmy. I don't mind."

Jimmy gestures his gratitude, while in his mind he asks himself. "What the fuck have I done?"

Can't Escape It

Jimmy's counselor is concerned about his unstable behavior during their last meeting. She calls him to come back to the office for another session. He begrudgingly agrees and arrives as scheduled.

"Thank you for coming in, Jimmy. It's good to see you." She opens his file and adjusts her notes. Jimmy takes a seat, looking down, not at Sandra, fidgeting with his hands.

"I asked you to come in so we can talk about our last session. It left me a little concerned. Are you feeling any better now?"

"Honestly," Jimmy begins. "I've been feeling worse. It's just... everything is so miserable. I don't even mind saying it anymore."

"I'm sorry to hear that. Can you tell me more about what's making you feel this way?"

"It's like there's this constant negative thing hanging over me. I can't escape it. I wake up every day and it's the same. What's the fuckin' point, ya know? I'm tired all the time. I don't even care about anything anymore. It's like I'm just going through the motions."

"That sounds exhausting. When you say you don't care about things, can you give me an example?"

"I shouldn't even say anymore. I'm not sure I ever cared about anything. My whole life, it's like I'm just... there."

Sandra nods, trying to assess Jimmy's frame of mind. "It sounds like you're feeling disconnected. How about your relationships? How are things with your family or friends?"

Jimmy shakes his head and looks away. "What people? I'm totally isolated. I'm a lousy father, a lousy everything. You keep saying I should reach out, I just can't." He fears sharing his thoughts fully would let loose feelings he could not control.

"But you're not all alone. Have you gone to any of the support meetings we talked about?"

"No, I didn't do that either." He answers with an attitude.

Jimmy's lack of alarm over his negative thoughts and behaviors is setting off red flags with Sandra. "It's common to feel like giving in when you're struggling with depression. It can make you feel like you're a burden, even though that's not true. Reaching out for support is a crucial step in managing these feelings."

Jimmy annoyed. "I know... I know what you said. I'm not depressed, I'm fucked."

Sandra attempts to be reassuring but sees it is not having any effect. "It's difficult to find the right words and to feel understood. Sometimes it helps to express those feelings here, where we can work through them together. "

"I don't even know what's bothering me. How am I going to tell you?!"

"Well, we can start identifying one small issue first and take it from there. We don't need to see the end of the tunnel right away. Or maybe a phone call or a message to someone you trust?" Sandra is trying to keep the situation relaxed.

"My wife hates me. I can't talk to her about anything. And the other one only wants me around to buy drugs." Jimmy stops talking for a moment. "I don't know, maybe I'll go to one of those group things."

"That sounds like a good step. Remember, it's okay to take things one step at a time. And if you need help drafting a message or thinking through what to say when you go, we can work on it together."

Jimmy nods, but there's no sign of relief in his expression. "Okay, I heard you, I'll try it."

"Good, I'm glad to hear it. And we'll continue to work on strategies to manage these feelings and help you feel more connected. You're not alone in this."

"Are we done now?"

"Not yet, Jimmy. We have some items to go through for the court."

The session continues with Sandra guiding Jimmy through some of the legal hurdles he must fulfill, coping strategies, and the next steps. After Jimmy leaves the session Sandra spends time thinking about his attitude and responses still feeling concerned. She considers alerting his parole officer about his deteriorating demeanor but decides it may be too early.

J immy keeps up with his work for Fat Lou, so at least he has money coming in, but the days turn into a tedious routine. Jimmy dislikes what he needs to do to get through the day and mainly the nights. It was an adventure for a few days, but the amusement is wearing off quickly and he does not like getting high in the car out in the open.

He decides it is time to reach out to Osana, he is not sure what to expect, but he knows he must make things right to get out of the car.

Jimmy picks up his phone and calls Osana's number. He can hardly remember the last time he was this nervous. He hangs on each ring hoping he does not get voicemail.

Finally, Osana answers. "Hello." Osana's voice was quiet, almost tentative.

"Hey babe." Jimmy trying to sound cheery. "It's me."

There is a long pause before Osana speaks again, her tone guarded. "I know that. What do you want, Jimmy?"

"I... I want to apologize," he pleads. "I know I messed up. I've been thinking about it a lot. I was stubborn and stupid, and I'm sorry for everything I said."

"Really? Just like that, huh?"

"I know what it sounds like, but I've been going to my sessions and thinking about things. I even went to some support group meetings." Jimmy fabricating what he thinks needs to be said has become effortless.

Osana sighs. "Jimmy, I don't even know where to start. The things you said and did... they're really fucked up."

"I know," I didn't mean them. I was just so wrapped up in my own bullshit that I didn't stop to think about what I was doing. I'm sorry. I should have handled it differently."

Jimmy could almost hear Osana planning her next words. "Jimmy, it's not just about the argument. Things are out of hand. I live here, ya know, it's not like a party house or anything."

"I'm realizing it," Jimmy admits. "I've been taking you for granted. I want to change that. I don't want to lose what we have going on."

Osana is in a predicament now. She feels bad for Jimmy but truly does not want to see him again at the same time. She knows Carlo will be back soon and needs to put a conclusive end to this relationship. Osana's voice has a trace of hesitation. "Well, maybe you can come back for a while, and we'll see what happens, ok?"

"I understand," Jimmy says sincerely. "And I'm willing to do whatever it takes. I'll start by making things right and showing you I can be better."

Osana has heard this before, but her heart is heavy for what she is going to do to him soon. "It's fine Jimmy. We'll see what happens."

"Yeah, I can respect that," Jimmy replies. "I just gotta do a couple of things and I can be there in a couple of hours."

"Oh no, not tonight. Come in the morning, but, not too early. How's that?"

This strikes Jimmy as a little odd, but does not want to jeopardize his moving back in. "Yeah, yeah, that's fine. I'm good for tonight anyway. I'll see you tomorrow."

"Thanks, I'll see you then. I gotta go now.

Jimmy feels a huge weight has been lifted off his shoulders, although he will spend one more night in the car. With a positive outlook, he decides to get something to eat, listen to the radio, and take it easy.

The Termination Letter

Marie's heart is sinking as she holds a letter from Jimmy's job. It was looking like a peaceful day with Bobby at school and Jeannie at home playing with her stuffed animals. That is all about to change.

She holds her breath as she opens it and is devastated by what she is reading. She immediately calls Jimmy, her hands trembling as she holds the phone. It rings a few times before Jimmy picks up. "Hey Marie, What's up?" Jimmy's tone is dull with fatigue underlying his words. He is no longer the same person, she can hear it in his voice.

"I got something in the mail today," Marie begins, her voice unsteady. "It's from the department."

There is a brief pause on the other end, Jimmy knows exactly what she received. "Oh yeah, what's it about?"

"It's a termination letter," her voice breaking. "They let you go."

Jimmy has to think of something quick to neutralize the situation. Marie can tell he is struggling to think of a lie fast enough. "What? That's crazy!" Jimmy pretends to be in disbelief. "Are you sure? Did you read it correctly?"

"I read it three times," Marie replies, tears welling in her eyes. "They said it's due to absenteeism and lateness, but Jimmy, you said you were still working. You're lying to me."

Jimmy's voice takes on a different tone—one of calm resolve. "Okay, let's not jump to conclusions. I'll make a couple of calls and figure this out. It's gotta be a mistake."

His words do nothing to calm her frayed nerves. "I'm just... I'm so upset. I thought you were at least still working."

"I have, really. I was just talking to my supervisor and he didn't say a word about it. I swear I straighten it out."

"I don't understand how you could do this to us." her voice cracking. "How are we going to live?"

"We will, Marie, I promise. It's just things haven't been—"

Marie's frame of mind was turning from shock to anger. "I don't believe a friggin' word you say, Jimmy! You've done nothing but lie to me lately, maybe for our whole marriage."

"C'mon Marie, that's not fair."

"Not fair?! You take off with some whore, do drugs, spend all your fuckin' family's money, now lose your job and you want to talk about fair? What am I going to do? Go on welfare?!"

"I kept up with all the shit I was supposed to do for all these years. What the fuck else you want?"

"I want you to be the husband and father you're supposed to be."

Jimmy is silent, he knows he is not going to prevail with her and his mind is so hazy he is having trouble coming up with more defenses.

"What do you want me to do with this letter? Are you coming to get it? I'll leave it in the mailbox downstairs for you."

"You know what, Marie, just burn the fuckin' thing. I don't give a shit what you do with it." And with that, Jimmy disconnects the call.

※※※

Jimmy arrives at Osana's with coffee and muffins to wake her up with a nice surprise and lets himself in. As he walks down the hall to the bedroom a muffled sound catches his ear. It is an unusual, almost imperceptible noise, then a thud followed by silence.

Jimmy's steps quicken as his instincts tell him something is wrong. In the bedroom, he finds Osana sprawled on the floor beside the bed, her face pale, her breathing shallow. Jimmy's blood runs cold as he thinks it could be an overdose.

Without a second thought, he kneels next to her, shaking her gently, calling her name. "Osana! Osana, wake up!" But her eyelids remain stubbornly closed and her body unresponsive. Panic surges through him, his hands tremble as he fumbles for his phone. He dials 911, his voice breaking as he speaks to the operator. "Please, my girlfriend... she's unconscious. I think she overdosed. I need help, now!"

The operator's voice is calm and steady, guiding Jimmy through the process while reassuring him help is on the way. As he follows the instructions, he keeps talking to Osana, his voice filled with desperation. "Hang in there, babe. Please, stay with me."

Minutes feel like hours. The sirens outside cut through the haze of his fear, and paramedics finally arrive. They work swiftly, their movements practiced and efficient. They take over from Jimmy's efforts, assess Osana's condition, and administer Narcan to counteract the effects of the possible overdose.

Jimmy stands dumbfounded; he has never witnessed such an episode in his life. The paramedics' faces are a blur as he watches them focus on Osana. "Is she going to die?" Jimmy asks the paramedics frantically.

"Not tonight, dude. We do this shit all the time."

Amy starts crying from all the commotion catching everyone's attention, including the paramedics. One of them turns to Jimmy. "Is there a baby in here?"

Jimmy takes a second. "Oh yeah, in the other room."

"Well, go take care of her!" The paramedic shouts at him.

"Oh, right." Jimmy heads to Amy's room. He picks her up and tries to get her to stop crying without any luck. He gets the idea to grab the baby bag and see if Elvie can help. Jimmy runs into the hallway and finds Elvie already there trying to find out what is happening.

"Elvie, I'm glad you're here. Can you help with Amy please?"

"Sure, Jimmy. Of course. What happened to Osana?"

"The paramedics are working on her now. We don't know yet."

Elvie knows that is a lie, but she takes the baby bag from Jimmy's arm, and he hands Amy to her. "Ok, go take care of Osana. I'll have Amy in my place until you're ready."

"Thank you so much, Elvie" Jimmy utters as he turns to get back to Osana.

Once back in the apartment, he stands at the bedroom door as the paramedics continue to work. He wonders what transpired after their phone call with her but has a very good idea.

Minutes later, Osana's eyes fluttered open, and she takes a shaky breath. Jimmy rushes to her side. "Babe, you're going to be okay."

Osana's gaze meets his, filled with confusion and fear. She struggles to speak, her voice a weak whisper. "Jimmy, I—"

"It's alright," he interrupts, squeezing her hand. "You're going to be alright. They're going to take care of you."

The paramedics inform Osana that she needs to go to the hospital for proper treatment, but she refuses. The paramedics look at Jimmy and he tries to convince her to go with them, but she insists she will not. "No! I ain't going anywhere. I'm fine now." She maintains but is obviously not well.

"But babe, you need to be checked out—"

"I'm staying right here. I don't know why you called them to begin with!" Osana says angrily, then asks Jimmy. "Where's Amy?"

"I brought her to Elvie's. She's watching her. Don't worry."

With that Osana closes her eyes and becomes limp.

"Is she ok?" Jimmy asks the paramedics.

"Yeah, she'll come around. She's going to sleep for a while now." They proceed to lift her up and place her on the bed. "Just let her sleep but keep an eye on her." The paramedics inform Jimmy they cannot take her against her will, so they give him some signs to look out for. If she exhibits any of them, she should be brought to the emergency room. With that they start packing up their equipment to head out of the apartment.

"Thank you, guys. We really appreciate it." Jimmy tells them. He returns to the bedroom to clean up the mess from all the turmoil. He picks the bedspread up from the floor and finds two used condoms and a bunch of crumpled paper towels. He stands there looking at them. "What a fuckin' jerk I am." He places everything in a plastic shopping bag and brings it to the trash cans in the basement. On his way back up he stops by Elvie's to see how she is doing with Amy. "Hey Elvie, I just want to see if everything's ok."

"We're fine, Jimmy. Don't worry about us. I'm kinda having fun watching her. Take your time."

"Great Thank you, Elvie."

"So... what happened to Osana?"

"What can I say. You've been around long enough."

Elvie touches his arm and gives me a caring look. "Just take care of her. We're just fine here. I even have a place for her to sleep, so take your time."

O sana wakes up hours later expecting Jimmy to be lying next to her, but she is alone. She goes into the living room and finds it topsy-turvy, empty beer cans thrown around and the television has a muted foreign movie on.

Jimmy is passed out on the couch, hair tousled and shirt untucked. Osana is still weak, but her face turns red with anger. She's had enough, and he needs to leave. She knows Jimmy has gathered what she was up to, but is at her limit with his disregard of her home. "Jimmy... Jimmy!" She calls out to him with no response. After several more times of calling his name, she shakes his shoulder forcefully and he slowly starts to come around.

"What? Who is, oh hey babe. "How are you feeling? I was so worried."

"Never mind how I feel! I told you I don't want this shit in my house."

"This shit? Look who's talking. Who was the ambulance here for, me or you?"

"This is my house. I'll do whatever the fuck I want."

"Believe me I know that." Jimmy mulls bringing up the condoms, but the exchange would turn too hostile. He does not want to get thrown out.

"I was stressed over what happened, so I had a few beers, that's all."

"A few beers? Is that my vape pen over there, broken?"

"Whatever. I'll buy you a new one."

"With that? You don't have any more money, asshole." Osana says insultingly.

"How could I forget – money, money, money, right?"

"No, it's not. I'm sick of you doing this. I can't do this anymore."

"Come on, babe. Look at what you just did. I wouldn't be overreacting if I were you." Jimmy's attempt to lessen the tension only backfires on him.

Osana's anger increases upon hearing that. "Oh, fuck you! It's almost every night with you. I'm tired of it, Jimmy. I'm so tired. It wasn't supposed to be like this! You're fuckin' everything up."

"So, I'm the fuck up? Who sat right here doing coke giving some old guy a blowjob? But I let it slide, right? And what about last night? You'd be dead right now if it wasn't for me."

"How many times did I let your shit slide? You keep saying it's the last time, but you just keep bullshitting me. Now get out!" Osana shouts.

"I'm trying, okay? I'm just... it's hard."

"You gotta straighten yourself out, not me. I don't want this here. You have to leave today, right now."

"You can't be serious. Where am I supposed to go?"

"I don't care! Go back to your wife. I don't want you here anymore."

Jimmy gets off the couch struggling to stand up. "You're just gonna throw me out? After everything I did for you?"

"You did this. I don't give a shit what you do, just do it somewhere else. How many times do I have to tell you? You're too fucked up to listen!"

Jimmy stands there, and the reality of her words sinks in. He looks around, then back at Osana, speaking in a much louder voice. "No, you know what? How much money have I given you? I'm not fuckin' leaving!"

"Be quiet! Amy's sleeping."

"She's next door, you stupid fuck. You don't even know where your kid is!"

This enrages Osana. "That's it! Get out or I'm calling the cops."

"Go ahead, who gives a fuck." As he sits back down on the couch.

Osana walks over to the kitchen table picks up her cellphone and dials 911. The dispatcher's professional voice contrasts sharply with Osana's anxious tone.

"911, what's your emergency?"

"Hi, um, I need help. I have a guy here... he's very angry, and he needs to leave my house. I can't handle him anymore and I'm afraid."

The dispatcher's voice softens with empathy. "Can you tell me more about what's happening? Is there immediate danger?"

"No, not right now, I think. He's just drunk and angry. I'm scared of what might happen if I keep telling him to leave."

"Alright, ma'am. I'm sending a unit to your address. It's important to stay calm and keep yourself safe. Is there anything else you need right now?"

"No, I'll wait for them."

Osana hangs up and takes a deep breath. But she steps back when she sees Jimmy get up from the couch again.

"You'd better stay over there!"

"You fuck! You really called them?"

"Yeah, Jimmy. I'm not taking your bullshit anymore. I told you to get out."

Both stand where they are, neither one of them is sure what to do at this point.

Two police officers arrive and knock on the door. Osana opens it, trying to steady her nerves. The officers are polite and professional, their presence both reassuring and intimidating.

Jimmy paces back and forth in the living room waiting for his turn to be addressed. One officer walks right up to him.

"What's going on, guy?" he asks with a stern voice.

"Not much." Jimmy tries to play everything off. "We had a little argument, that's all."

"It sounds like it was more than that." The officer comes back with.

"Well, I don't know—"

"You been drinking? You got a strong smell of alcohol coming off you." The officer asks decisively.

"A few beers, that's all."

"C'mon dude, tell me the truth. You did more than drink."

Jimmy stammers trying to get a reasonable excuse out until the officer speaks again.

"Listen, I don't give a shit. We're here to defuse the situation. Everyone must remain calm. Can we help you find a place to stay for tonight, because she wants you to go."

"I think if I can talk to her—" Jimmy almost begging. He does not want to be without a roof over his head.

"Dude, that ain't happening. You can't stay here. You seem like a reasonable guy, let's not escalate this."

"Make him give me back my keys before he goes." Osana demands from the officer.

"Dude, you got her keys?"

"Not on me. I don't know where they are, probably in my car." Jimmy says as he pats down his own pockets.

"He don't have them." The officer says to Osana, then turning to Jimmy. "Listen, if you find them, don't be an idiot and try to come back here. You will be arrested."

Jimmy's shoulders slump in resignation. He knows there is no point in arguing. He turns to Osana, his voice soft but strained. "I didn't realize what I was doing."

"I didn't want this." Osana replies, feeling sorry for him.

The officers watch as Jimmy gathers a few belongings and he stumbles towards the door, pausing for a moment to glance back at Osana.

As the door closes behind him and the officers, Osana feels awful about having to do that. She sits in the kitchen burying her face in her hands. It is a relief to have him out of her way, but it does not address the situation with Carlo.

# What's Real Anymore

J immy is in a desperate position with nowhere to live and not enough money. He thinks of where he can find money and valuables – his own apartment. So, he devises a plan to call from a nearby payphone to see if anyone is home. If no one answers he will sneak in and take what he can. While inside he will break a window and toss some items around to make it look like a standard burglary.

He waits until he believes Marie will either be bringing their son to school or at a doctor's appointment with the baby. He finds a payphone and calls with no answer, so he makes his way to the apartment. He approaches the building carefully not to be seen by any of the neighbors.

Once comfortable he makes his way upstairs and tiptoes into the apartment. It is so quiet he can hear his heart pounding in his chest. He moves cautiously, aware that any noise could alert a neighbor.

He already knows where the valuables are, so he doesn't need much time. He goes into the kitchen and opens the cabinet where Marie keeps the food money and takes it. Then into the bedroom and grabs Marie's jewelry out of her dresser drawer.

He looks in her closet to see if there is anything she is hiding but finds nothing. He figures he has around one thousand dollars worth of items, so it is time to go. A wave of guilt sweeps over him as he exits the building, but it quickly fades.

He is set with the cash but needs to find a place to sell the jewelry. He thinks of a pawn shop back at Hunts Point, so he heads there next. Counting the money in his car, Jimmy is able to walk away with about seven hundred dollars.

❋❋❋

As friends, Mark and Danny decide it is time to reach out to Jimmy to offer assistance to him or his family. They agree a call from Danny will be less pressure than if Mark calls, but it will be in Mark's presence, so he can listen in. Danny takes his phone out and calls Jimmy.

Jimmy stares at the phone on the seat next to him until it nearly goes to voicemail. Knowing it is Danny calling he gauges the likely direction this conversation will go. He eventually answers acting as if everything is fine. "Hey, Danny! How ya doing, man?"

"Jimmy, my man, I'm good. What about you?"

"Ya know, same shit, different day. It's good to hear from you."

"I'm happy to hear your voice, too. I just wanted to check in to see how you're doing."

"Yeah, everything's great. Hanging in there."

Danny looks at Mark, and they seem to have the same view - Danny should get to the point. "Don't bullshit your old buddy Danny like that. C'mon lad, what's going on?"

It has been a while since they spoke, and the awkwardness of his situation distresses Jimmy. "To be honest, things aren't great right now, but I'm trying to get back on track. It's just taking some time."

"Are you getting any help with... well... the drugs?"

"Oh yeah, I've been seeing a counselor and going to meetings. It's been helping me a lot." Jimmy continues the charade.

"Are you back home?"

"Not yet. Marie and I have been talking more lately and we're working things out. I'll probably be home in a few weeks. She just wants me to do some more of the sessions and meetings."

"That's good. The little ones ok? I still pray for Jeannie every day."

"It's about status quo. The doctors are hopeful they'll come up with a treatment before long. But, ya know, everybody's pretty good."

"I'm glad to hear it. I hope you're back to your normal self soon, too. You got a great life, Jimmy, with Marie and the kids and all. And we'll all help you find work again once you get to that point."

"Thanks, Danny. It means a lot." Jimmy sees this as an opportunity to extract cash from Danny. "Hey Danny, I'm in a bit of a bind, to tell you the truth. Things have been rough lately. I could use some help."

"Help? What kind of help?" Danny's tone shifts from concern to curiosity.

"I don't have enough to cover the bills this month. The landlord's breathing down our necks and we're getting collection letters from the doctors and all. I hate to ask, but I could use some cash." playing on Danny's sympathy. "Can you help me out?"

There is a long pause on the other end of the line. Red flags are being raised in Danny's mind. "I had an idea that might be the case," Danny says in a soft but firm voice. "How much are we talking about?"

"Two thousand dollars. I know it's a lot. I wouldn't ask if I didn't need it."

Danny exhales slowly. "Is that what you really need it for, or are you gonna spend it on other shit?"

"No, seriously Danny, that's what I need it for. I wouldn't give you a story about it."

"Listen, my friend, I know you got a long road ahead of you, so maybe, if it's ok with you, we'll reach out to Marie and we'll get her and the kids some relief."

"I think it would help with my situation with her if she thought the money was coming from me. I don't want her knowing I had to take a handout from anyone."

"I don't know, Jimmy. It sounds kind of off to me. I think it's better to go straight to Marie. We'd feel better about it. I just want the help going to the ones that need it, ok?"

"Danny, I swear that's what I'm going to do with it. I'm not fuckin' around. It's better my way. I'll pay you back real soon. You don't have to worry about it.

Danny looks at Mark who is shaking his head strongly in the negative. Danny braces himself and gets back to Jimmy. "Listen, we want to help, but we just can't give you any money right now. If we do it, it's got to go straight to Marie."

"Who's this 'we' you keep saying?"

"Ya know, maybe me and Mark and whoever."

This irritates Jimmy, his scheme is not working causing him to lose control with Danny. "I can't fuckin' believe you! I'm telling the truth. I need the money going to me, not fuckin' Marie! If you don't want to help, then go fuck yourself. I got other ways of making money."

"Jimmy, calm down. We're talking—

Jimmy ends the call.

Danny looks at Mark with real sorrow in his eyes. "Well, that didn't go the way we had hoped."

"I know how you feel. He's really out there. He's got to hit bottom before anyone can help him."

"You're right. I've known many people who went through this with drinking. He's in the thick of it. I know he doesn't mean to bullshit me, it's the drugs making him do it."

※ ※ ※

After the call, Jimmy wanders around thinking of a way to get more money to feed his habit. The call with Danny has already been completely scrubbed from his memory. It is a dead end; no sense to dwell on it.

He sits alone for a long time with the noise of vehicles rushing by seems to help him focus inward. He rubs his temples, frustration etched deeply into his features. "Why does everything always have to go wrong? I'm such a fuckin' loser." he mutters. "I'm just stumbling from one disaster to the next. I have nothing, I am nothing. Nobody gives a shit about me, they never did."

"Oh fuck!" Jimmy remembers he has an appointment with his counselor today. His parole officer warned about missing them and he does not want to be locked up for a petty infraction. He gets to his vehicle and drives over to her office. Today he's feeling a mix of anger and despair; his mind is a mess making it difficult to think straight.

The next thing he realizes is he is in Sandra's office and becomes aware of the conversation when Sandra pokes his leg to get his attention.

"Jimmy, is everything all right?"

"Yeah, Sandra, I'm ok. I was just thinking of something."

"I was just asking how you felt these sessions were going."

Jimmy pauses for a second and then in a low voice avoiding eye contact says. "I don't think this is working."

Sandra is concerned, leaning forward slightly, and asks him why he thinks that.

Jimmy fidgets with his hands, eyes still fixed on the floor. "I feel worse, honestly. Like, every time we talk, I walk out of here feeling more tangled up than when I came in. I thought this was supposed to help, but—"

"Jim, it's not uncommon for therapy to feel challenging at times. Can you describe a specific instance where you felt things got worse?"

Jimmy looks up briefly, then looks away again. "It's like... every time we dig into something, it just makes everything seem more messed up. I start thinking about things more, and I get more fucked up. Last week, after our session, I couldn't sleep for days. I kept replaying everything we talked about."

"It sounds like you're experiencing a lot of apprehension. Sometimes, exploring painful topics can bring up difficult emotions. But it's important to assess whether this approach is working for you. There are only professionals I can refer you to if needed." Sandra advises him.

"I don't even know what's real anymore. I keep questioning if I'm making any progress. Sometimes I think I should just stop coming. Maybe I'm just not cut out for this."

"I hear your frustration. This isn't always a smooth process. It's a journey that can have bumps along the way. But your feelings are valid, and we can work together to address them. And let's not forget the court-mandated you to come to these sessions."

Jimmy is now agitated. "Yeah, I know all about the court and my arrest and the drugs and the guys in the cell and all. I know."

"Jimmy, I know you've been through a lot lately and you might be feeling a bit disoriented, but we can explore other strategies or techniques. It's crucial that you feel like this is working for you. Let's take some time to discuss what might be more effective or what might be missing in our current approach.

"Nothing's going to work for me. It's too late."

"That's not true. We just need to find a path that feels right for you. Let's work together to make this a more supportive experience."

"Listen, I know you get paid to say certain things to the people they force to come here, but it's not for me. I got my own plan to resolve this."

Sandra is now very concerned. "Jimmy, what are you talking about? You have to tell me what you're thinking."

Jimmy looks Sandra straight in the eye for what seems like a very long time, then walks out of the office. Sandra immediately gets on the phone with his parole officer telling him that Jimmy is growing more unstable. She feels he might be planning something violent against himself or someone else. The officer says he is backed up with other pressing cases currently, but will note it and follow up on it as soon as he can.

Carlo's On His Way

O sana is pacing around her living room. She has a very clear objective – Jimmy has to get out of her life permanently before Carlo returns. She has been rehearsing this conversation in her mind numerous times, but the moment has come. She knows Jimmy's mental state is not that of a rational person, so this news could cause him to become unhinged. She is prepared to call 911 again if she has to.

Jimmy sits in his car thinking about Osana and how he needs to get back with her. He decides to call and plead for forgiveness. He gives her a bogus story about talking to his counselor, understanding himself better, and going to support groups. Osana does not believe him but realizes she needs to have a conversation with him about Carlo, so she allows him to come over.

Jimmy shows up at her apartment a short while later with a large pizza and soda and places it all on the kitchen table. His mind is still not completely settled from the session.

"C'mon, let's eat!" Jimmy appears to be doing his best to not let on he is brutally troubled at the time. He looks up when Osana's pacing grows more intense, a crease forming on his forehead. "Babe, you okay?"

Osana stops mid-stride, her heart pounding. "Jimmy, I got some news I gotta tell you about."

He sets his pizza down and sits up straight. "Sure, what's up?"

She tries to steady her nerves. "There's something I haven't told you about, and it's time I did.

Jimmy wearily. "What now? What's going on?"

Osana's eyes look everywhere but at Jimmy. "Amy's father is out of prison."

The room falls silent, her words hang in the air between them. Jimmy's face tightens, and he leans forward, his voice strains. "Is that good or bad? What's it mean for us?"

Osana nervously pours herself a glass of soda. "I mean, it's only because he got arrested that we separated. I didn't leave him or anything, and he is Amy's father. My feelings for him never really went away."

Jimmy's eyes widen. "So, I still don't understand." His mind is so muddled he is having issues absorbing how an authentic relationship functions.

"He's in Texas right now, but he'll be back here soon. And he's going to live here."

The silence that follows is deafening. Jimmy stands up, his face pale. "You're serious, aren't you?"

Osana nods. "I'm sorry, Jimmy. I don't want to hurt you; you know how I feel about you, but I just gotta do this."

Jimmy tries to keep his composure. "You could have said something before."

Osana's eyes fill with tears. "I know. I didn't know what else to do. I wasn't even sure he was ever coming back. You and me had fun, don't ruin it now."

Jimmy's shoulders slump. "So, what now?"

"We still have some time," Osana says softly. "Let's just make the best of it." Osana notices a change in Jimmy's face and demeanor, like a switch flipped in his head. She is skeptical but hopes it is a sign he is accepting the situation.

"Yeah, you know what? You're right. I guess that's it." Jimmy says slowly. "You gonna have a slice or what? It's getting cold."

After eating Osana stands and begins gathering items from the table to clean the kitchen up. "You done eating, babe?"

Jimmy takes his last bite of pizza. "Yeah, I ate four slices. I am stuffed. I'm going to lay down inside for a while."

"Good, you must be sleepy after all that. I'm going to throw all this stuff out downstairs. I don't want to get roaches." Osana finishes clearing the table and puts everything in a garbage bag. She goes down and places it in the building's trash cans.

On her way back up she runs into Elvie in the hallway, like she was waiting for Osana. Elvie is worried after the ambulance incident and wants to offer her support. Elvie has half a chocolate cake and a well-worn journal with her. "Hi, Osana!" Elvie greets her.

"Oh hi, Elvie. What do you got there?" Osana looks at Elvie with curiosity.

Elvie smiles warmly. "I was in the mood for some chocolate cake, but I'll eat the whole thing if I keep it with me, so I'm trying to save myself! Would you like half?"

Osana chuckles. "Ok, I know the feeling. Um, would you like to come in?" Osana is reluctant to invite her, but it seems like the right thing to do.

Elvie signals her agreement and the two of them walk into Osana's apartment and sit at the kitchen table.

"Would you like some tea?" Osana offers.

"Sure, that would be nice. Whatever you have is good. To be honest, the cake is not the only reason I wanted to see you. You know I was around when the ambulance and all happened." Elvie confesses.

"I know. I am so thankful for what you did for Amy that night."

"I believe everyone deserves a chance. I know it's not much, but I thought you might like a bit of encouragement."

Elvie looks around the apartment and sees it was a stark reflection of Osana's struggle—disarrayed and dimly lit. Elvie sets the journal on the table and gently encourages Osana to have a look. It is a written record of Elvie's life—of her struggles, her triumphs, and the people who had helped her along the way.

"Sometimes," Elvie says, "we need someone to believe in us when we've lost belief in ourselves."

Osana flips through reading random pages. The walls she has built around herself start to crumble seeing what Elvie has been through in her life. It's a story so similar to hers she cannot help but be touched by it. A tale of a young woman who once dreamed of doing something with her life but lost her way, merely holding onto a faint flicker of old aspirations. She talks to Osana about support groups and counseling services she could connect her with.

Osana initially rejects what Elvie is saying to her but breaks down after they talk for a while. Tears come to Osana's eyes, but a beam to Elvie's face knowing she had broken through. "You've taken the most important step," she says. "You've shown you're stronger than you think."

"I'm just tired, so tired. I feel like it's time for a change." Osana says wiping the tears from her face.

"I know exactly how you feel, Osana. We all need to get to that point before something positive happens."

"Yeah, I think I'm there. I want to be a good mother and all but can't get away from some old habits."

"And that's fine. We meet people where they are. Can I invite you to our next meeting?"

"I would like that."

Elvie and Osana hug for an extended time and finish their tea and cake.

At the entrance door as Elvie prepares to leave Osana expresses her thanks for Elvie coming by and how she is going to take her offers of help seriously.

"I'm so glad to hear you say that. Remember I'm only next door if you ever need help or just want to talk." Elvie reminds her.

As Elvie exits the apartment Jimmy comes walking out of the bedroom.

"Oh no, what are you two up to?" Jimmy says playfully.

"Nothing bad, Jimmy. Elvie just brought me some cake and we were talking."

"Oh cool. That's nice."

Elvie continues down to her apartment and Jimmy and Osana walk back to the kitchen area to check out the cake.

"How is she? I don't really know her." Jimmy inquires.

"She's very nice. I never spoke to her much, but today we had a good conversation. She likes to deal with people."

"Why? You need dealing with?"

"Maybe not me so much. She volunteers for women's groups and stuff like that. She's been around and wants to help women get their lives back on track, that's all."

"Maybe she can get you back to painting." Jimmy says as he points to Osana's artwork.

"Maybe. I haven't picked up a brush in years. I almost forgot what it feels like to paint something just for the sake of painting it."

Jimmy puts his arm around Osana's shoulders. "I don't think it's something you can forget. It's just inside you, ready to come out whenever you're ready to let it."

Osana's eyes move down to look at the floor. "Sometimes I wonder if I should have kept up with it, you know? If things might have been different."

Jimmy squeezes her shoulders tighter. "You could have been a great painter, babe. Look at the talent you have. Your work is something special, something real. But life put you on a different path, and you gotta respect that. Like my life changed and put me on a path I gotta do now."

"Oh yeah? What do you have to do now?"

Jimmy ignores the question and continues. "But what if you could still do something with it? I mean, you haven't tried in a long time."

"I wouldn't even know where to start," she admits, her voice a whisper.

Jimmy's smile widens. "I know where to start." He walks over to the closet where he tossed the painting supplies. Once he gathers them all together, he brings them over to Osana. "Why not set up an area over in the corner and see what happens?"

A tear slides down Osana's cheek, and she feels a sense of encouragement. She believes her art could find its way back into her life, not as a regret of the past, but as a promise of the future. Together, they clear the corner of the room, transforming it into a space for Osana's creativity.

She sits looking at the paint and brushes for a while. "Thanks, Jimmy. I appreciate it."

"Ya know, I think you're the only one I ever really loved. I'm going to miss you."

Osana looks at him with compassion and sympathy. "I'm gonna miss your skinny ass, too."

They hug and kiss, making Jimmy highly emotional. He thanks Osana for her sympathy and excuses himself. Osana goes to check on Amy and Jimmy heads to the bathroom.

A Strange Sense

Jimmy sits in the bathroom on the verge of tears wondering how this is all affecting his children and decides to call home. "Hey, Marie. It's me, Jimmy." He says in almost a whisper.

"I know who it is."

"I know you're upset with me, but I was wondering how the kids were doing. Is Jeannie ok? And Bobby?"

"Bobby's doing fine. He enjoys school."

"Does he ask about me?"

"Not really, but I sat him down and gave him some story about where you are."

"Thanks for that, Marie." Jimmy says sincerely.

"Don't thank me. I didn't do it for you. I was worried about him. And, to tell you the truth, he doesn't even seem to miss you."

This hits Jimmy to his very soul but holds back his tears and continues. "What about Jeannie? Do they know anything yet?"

"She's here with me. The doctor says something like a virus might be attacking her heart, but they can't seem to pinpoint it yet. It's going to take more time."

"Hey, whatever she needs, just let me know."

"She needs health insurance, Jimmy, but you took care of that, didn't you?"

Jimmy knows she's right and doesn't quite know how to reply. "I'm working on appealing my termination with the union and trying to find other work in the meantime, Marie." Jimmy knows there is no hope of ever getting his sanitation job back and is not even trying.

"You shouldn't have screwed things up to begin with, especially over some whore!"

Marie breaks down, crying hysterically. "How could you do this to us, Jimmy?! Things weren't great, but we didn't deserve this! Anything's ruined now!"

"I'm sorry, Marie. It'll be over soon, I swear." Jimmy can sense he is nearing his point of no return.

"And on top of everything else the apartment was broken into."

"Oh shit, really? Did they get a lot of stuff?

"The cash I had hidden and most of my jewelry."

"Did you call the police?"

"Of course I did. But what are they going to do?"

"So, they have no suspects or anything, right?" Jimmy asks curiously.

"No, nobody. There's not even a fingerprint to go on."

"Well, if you need anything, just let me know."

"And what are you going to do? You're worthless to us, a fucking failure and I don't believe a word you say!" Marie slams the phone down.

Jimmy's fury reaches a crescendo, he is a storm of frustration. He stands staring daggers at himself in the bathroom mirror when something peculiar happens. The familiar world around him seems to distort and waver. The walls of his bathroom melt away, and Jimmy feels an inexplicable pull towards an unfamiliar sensation.

In a blink, Jimmy finds himself standing among the trees in one of Osana's paintings. He feels the crisp air and the grass soft beneath his feet. The forest is silent except for the gentle rustling of leaves and the distant hum of crickets. Jimmy looks around, bewildered, his anger forgotten.

He sits down on a smooth rock, feeling the cool surface against his skin. The stillness of the woods is a stark contrast to the chaos he left behind. Jimmy's breathing slows as he takes in the scene before him. The sky is a gradient of oranges and blues, and the clouds drift lazily by, their movements synchronizing with his calming breath.

A strange sense of tranquility washes over him. The usual tension in his shoulders eases, and the clenching of his jaw relaxes. For the first time in what feels like forever, Jimmy is not burdened by his frustrations. The serenity of the meadow seeps into him, and his mind, once crowded with anger, finds space to breathe.

As he sits there, Jimmy's mind drifts, free from the chains of his former rage. Thoughts that once seemed like insurmountable obstacles now appear trivial. He senses he is outside of time itself, feeling a profound sense of peace. Only a loud knocking on the door brings him back to the present.

"Jimmy, how long are you going to be in there?" Osana exclaims.

It takes Jimmy a moment to regain his thoughts. "I'm coming out now." He says as he leaves the bathroom.

Osana looks at him oddly. "What the hell were you doing in there for so long?"

"Nothing really." Jimmy says calmly. "You know what? I gotta do some shopping."

"Shopping? Shopping for what?"

"We're gonna have a special night at home. How's that sound?"

"I ain't cooking, if that's what you mean." Osana tells him half-jokingly.

"No, no I'll do everything. Leave it to me."

With that Jimmy takes his car keys and leaves the apartment.

***

"Babe, I'm back!" Jimmy walks into the kitchen putting several bags of groceries down on the table.

Osana walks in from the other room and starts looking through the bags. "That's a lot of stuff."

"Yep, for something that never was or will be."

"What's that supposed to mean?"

"We're gonna have a special night. I'm going to cook us a great dinner, a rosemary chicken, risotto, and sauteed broccoli rabe, and we can watch a good movie after that." Jimmy pulls two bottles of wine out of a bag. "I know you're going to want these!"

"Ooh, my favorite. Anything else?"

Jimmy knows she's referring to drugs. "Nope. You won't need anything else."

"Can I get a glass of wine then?"

"Nope again, baby. Wait 'til dinner."

"Since when do you know how to cook?"

"I used to cook at home all the time. I would watch my mother and just picked it up."

Osana is curious about his all of a sudden upbeat mood as she goes to the baby's room.

"Hey babe, when you're done with the baby can you set the table? I'll start on the chicken and risotto."

"Ok, but you gotta pay me in wine!" Osana teases.

"Deal, no problem."

"Should I see if Elvie is available to watch Amy?"

"No, it's fine. That won't be necessary." Jimmy utters and gets back to cooking.

Osana thinks this is odd but finishes putting out dishes and silverware in the dining area. She feels a sense of comfort as she hears the clinking of pots and pans. She goes back into the living room to relax when done with the table.

Jimmy surprises her by bringing her a glass of wine as she watches television. "Here you go, ma'am. Your payment for setting the table!"

"Thank you. How nice."

"Oh, and can you make sure the DVD player is working? We'll need it for the movie later."

"We just used it the other night, it's fine."

"Please just check it for me. It's important." Jimmy asks kindly.

"What's so fuckin' important about a DVD?" Osana mumbles to herself.

As Jimmy walks back to the kitchen he says, "Dinner will be ready soon." over his shoulder.

Osana slips a DVD into the player, and everything is working well. After a while, Jimmy leans into the living room and announces.

After some time of Jimmy scampering around the kitchen he announces. "Dinner's ready! Come sit."

Osana walks over and is impressed with the dinner he has made.

"Wow, everything looks so good. I can't wait to taste it."

"Well, you know all the best chefs are men, right?"

"Haha, very funny!"

"No, it's true. You never heard of Wolfgang Puck or Gordon Ramsey or Emeril Lagasse? All men!"

"Yeah, Emeril, the bam! guy."

"Exactly. Here let me serve you."

"Such good service. You're gonna spoil me."

"Ok with me." says Jimmy. "I want this to feel like a real home. I'm really glad I moved in with you.

"Jimmy, you know we talked about—"

"You want a leg or white meat?"

This sort of denial concerns Osana, but she thinks he doesn't want to ruin the day, so she keeps quiet.

"A leg is good. It's been nice having you around." sipping her wine.

"I was wondering, what would be a great vacation for you?"

"I don't know. I guess Hawaii." Osana muses.

"Oh yeah, Hawaii would be great. Imagine enjoying the sun and beaches there? And you can see volcanoes, too. I'm more inclined towards somewhere with mountains. Maybe a cabin in the woods. What do you think?"

"Sure, that'd be nice, too."

"Yeah, but there's no time."

Osana reflects. "You take me back Jimmy. When I was a kid, we went on a family picnic to one of those parks upstate. My aunts and uncles were there, and my mother even got my grandmother to come. We had fun that day.

"Sounds like a good time."

"It was. Oh, but I lost my necklace that day. It had a gold heart on it, too. I felt so bad."

"Sometimes you lose things and there's no way to ever get them back."

Osana wonders at the odd sort of tone Jimmy says that in. The wine is taking its effect on her, so the impression only stays with her briefly.

Jimmy continues. "So, what's your favorite thing about our place right now?"

Osana is truly getting worried by his use of 'our place.' "Oh, I love how cozy it feels. Like, it's nice to be home and just relax.

Jimmy reaches out and takes Osana's hand, squeezing it softly "I agree. It's like our little sanctuary."

The word 'sanctuary' reminds her of the words she said when she first moved into the apartment. This space was to be for her baby and herself. Everything else, especially anything involving a man, was to take place outside these walls. She is annoyed at herself because somehow her addictions and loneliness made her forget this promise.

Jimmy spends the rest of the meal with his head down, not saying one word, until looking up. "You done eating?" he asks as he stands up.

Osana leans back in her chair, rubbing her belly. "I'm so full."

"Excellent. I hope you enjoyed everything."

"It was all delicious, I'm impressed. I didn't know you were such a good cook."

"Chef, Osana, I'm a good chef." Jimmy laughs.

"Right, I'm sorry."

Jimmy proceeds to clear the table putting everything by the sink, except for the one remaining bottle of wine and two wine glasses which he places on the coffee table in the living room.

"Is Amy all set? We gotta get ready for movie night."

"Yeah, she's all fed and in her crib sleeping. She should be good for a while."

"Great. I got us Swiss Family Robinson movie." Jimmy tells her as he pulls a DVD from a small bag.

"What the hell is that?"

"You never saw it? It's about a family that gets shipwrecked on a deserted island. They build a home and learn how to survive while they wait to be rescued. They all love and help each other to live. It's a classic."

"It doesn't sound like it, but ok." Osana says doubtfully.

"There's no big explosions or gunfights if that's what you're looking for."

"Ha, very funny."

Jimmy puts the DVD in, hits play, and sits on the couch next to Osana, putting his arm around her. "You're about to experience cinematic history."

"You think I'm going to like a movie from a hundred years ago?

"It's not a hundred years old and it's not just the movie, it has a certain message."

"All right, you seem excited about it."

They settle in as the movie starts. Jimmy's eyes are glued to the screen throughout the film and Osana spends most of her time on her phone and occasionally checking on Amy. The credits finally start to roll on the screen. Osana is relieved; Jimmy is still animated.

"How'd like the cinematography, it's just brilliant."

"The what?"

"They had to be so creative with their techniques because they didn't have all the special effects we have today."

Jimmy's face suddenly turns intense. "Why can't families be like that now? People just loving and helping each other. Why?"

"Jimmy, relax it's just a movie." Osana becomes increasingly alarmed.

"Today everything is shit. Nobody gives a fuck anymore. You lose everything and they send you to some asshole telling you stupid shit with a bunch of fuckin' posters on her walls." Jimmy's entire demeanor is altered, and his voice is harsh.

Osana is thoroughly afraid now. Jimmy has become unhinged from being a calm, positive person just a short time ago. She tries to scale back his reactions. "Ok, take it easy babe. Why don't you get us some more wine and we'll talk."

"There's no more wine, we drank it." Jimmy informs her.

"That's fine. Go in the bedroom and get the vape. We'll do a few hits off that and loosen up." Osana still trying to de-escalate the situation.

"I got a better idea." Jimmy states as he lifts himself up.

"Yeah, ok whatever you need." Osana wonders what he could be talking about.

Jimmy walks to the back of the apartment as Osana waits. He's gone for longer than expected but she figures he's trying to calm himself before returning. He returns to the living room and stands at the end of the couch where Osana is sitting. He has the vape pen in his left hand and the .38 handgun Fat Lou gave him in his right behind his back.

"Here ya go, babe." as he hands Osana the vape pen.

She takes it. "Thanks. Aren't you going to sit?"

"I just wanted to feel love... I'm sorry."

"What are you sorry for now?"

Elvie jumps from the recliner in her apartment as she hears a gunshot, and another a few seconds later. She can hear baby Amy begin to cry.

Mental Health and Substance Abuse Help

I f you or someone you know needs assistance with any of these issues, please do not hesitate to reach out to one of these groups or a local resource. Help is out there, you just need to reach out for it!

* In life-threatening situations, call 911 or go to the nearest emergency room.

* If you are suicidal or in emotional distress, consider using the 988 Suicide & Crisis Lifeline.

* Call or text 988 or chat online at chat.988lifeline.org to connect with a trained crisis counselor. The Lifeline provides 24-hour, confidential support to anyone in suicidal crisis or emotional distress. You can reach a specialized LGBTQI+ affirming counselor by texting "Q" to 988 or by calling 988 and pressing "3."

* If you are a veteran, consider using the Veterans Crisis Line. Call 988, then press "1." You can also text 838255 or chat online. The Veterans Crisis Line is a 24-hour,

confidential resource that connects veterans with a trained responder. The service is available to all veterans and those who support them, even if they are not registered with the VA or enrolled in VA healthcare.

- Millions of Americans have mental and substance use disorders. You can find treatment at findtreatment.gov. Substance Use and Mental Health Treatment Locator. To find treatment facilities confidentially, 24/7, please call 1-800-662-4357 (HELP).

- National Child Abuse Hotline: If you suspect a child has been harmed by abuse or neglect, please call 1-800-422-4453.

- Substance Use: Whether you are looking for help for yourself, worried about someone else, or looking to partner with 211, start here to learn more about available mental health and substance use resources and services. The Substance Abuse and Mental Health Administration (SAMHSA) operates a free helpline to provide people with answers about common mental health conditions, including substance abuse disorders. The helpline can also help people navigate treatment options. Call 1-800-622-4357.

- The National Drug Helpline at (844) 289-0879 is a free, confidential, 24/7 drug and alcohol hotline.

- National Drug and Alcohol Treatment Hotline: 1-800-662-HELP (4357).

- Alcoholics Anonymous: https://www.aa.org/

- Crisis Text Line Text HOME to 741741 from anywhere

in the United States – 24/7, free, confidential. Crisis Text Line (CTL) is here for you. A live, trained volunteer Crisis Counselor receives the text and responds, all from our secure online platform. The volunteer Crisis Counselor will help you move from a hot moment to a cool calm.

- Gamblers Anonymous: to find someone to talk to and a meeting near you. gamblersanonymous.org

- Narcotics Anonymous: https://na.org/

- National Domestic Violence Hotline: 1.800.799.SAFE (7233) or Text "START" to 88788.

- National Network of Depression Centers List of resources: https://nndc.org/resource-links/

- The Mental Health Hotline: 866-903-3787 can answer your questions confidentially and free of charge.